KATY AND THE EMERALD

G000116432

Rena Knox

To my wonderful soulmate Brian, who passed away in 2019, and who encouraged me and put up with me spending many hours of writing - love you forever.

To my many grandchildren and great-grandchildren who brought out my inner child, never judged me, and also showed lots of unconditional love - bless them.

To my beautiful granddaughter and friend, Sarah, who created the front cover illustration -many thanks.

And last but not least, to my friend Yvonne who gave me confidence over the years. She passed me a writing pad and a pen on visiting me in hospital. This kind act inspired me to write this book. No grapes for me! She knows me well.

Yvonne, my guiding light - thank you.

About the Author
Doreen M Marsden

Born in Liverpool in 1943, I moved to the countryside in Scotland at a young age, then to Glasgow Town at fourteen. On leaving school, I achieved five o-levels and could have gone further with my education, however, I married at just over sixteen years of age and had my five children within 8 years. I moved back to England in 1962 and I now live on the borders of Derbyshire, at the foot of the Pennine Hills. I eventually worked in wages and accounts then became a Civil Servant (so boring).

At fifty, my life changed after an awakening through meditation which unleashed lots of creative abilities and confidence in me.

At fifty, I embarked on music lessons and got as far as the third grade, enough for me to put a song together as I'd had an ear for music since being a child.

I pursued new age therapies, i.e., massage and reflexology, and through spiritual healing, became a Reiki Master and created workshops teaching about the body's subtle chakras and Reiki. On retirement, I eventually became a voluntary worker in the local community offering my healing therapies to those who were in pain.

Unfortunately, in 2013, my husband was diagnosed with Alzheimer's. That chapter of my life ended as his did. Brian sadly passed away in 2019, bless him. I have tweaked my book, which I first wrote in 2006, and now that it is finished, I have embarked on my second book as I have got the writer's bug now.

My motto: Life is what you make it.

Synopsis

Katy was a two-year-old child from hell. She was an old soul and, unbeknown to her, carried old, destructive karma that she found hard to deal with, taking it out on her brother and sister, James and Dione. The girl with the cruel streak nearly lost them their home, and her parents, David and Nat, struggled to keep her under control and were at their wit's end when David's Aunt Agatha turned up after many years of living in Africa. Agatha had many new age gifts of healing scrying with the crystal ball and counselling those who needed help. She was also a psychic, and through these gifts, she had the intuition to know that the family needed her help.

The aunt bonded with Katy immediately and there was a big change in this toddler.

The elderly lady brought health, wealth and happiness to the Bex Family for many years, however, when her health deteriorated, their whole lives were turned upside down.

A necklace that Agatha wore permanently was removed by Katy when her aunt was ill and this eventually changed the course of Katy's life. She became the child from hell again and her mind, body and spirit felt that it was once more on trial. Katy, now nine, found solace in her aunt's healing room, called Angel's Den, and one night, she found herself propelled into the higher realms of another planet, making new friends, Dominic the Monk, who was Keeper of Dreams and Guardian of the Crystal Caves, Art, the musical clown, Silky, the spider and many creatures in the Forest of Shadows helping them to find the rainbow colours while seeking out Grabb the Jackdaw, who stole the precious necklace that Katy was on the verge of giving to Dominic the Monk.

This was a journey she had to make without choice as this planet was dying and her aunt's Emerald Key held the answer.

Agatha, who was in spirit, watched over her from the Planet of Light with a lovely magician called Magi. They watched from a distance as Katy and her friends had to go through trials, tribulations and danger to bring light back to the planet as the Hucan and his warriors, the Huccanites, fed on darkness and destroyed all who stood in their way. Pupils at her school who, at first, were unaware that she was missing, were plotting their revenge, especially Sadie Frost, who tried to bully Katy's best friend, Claire, into stealing an ancient book which had belonged to her Aunt Agatha. Her parents on the Earth plane were devastated at Katy's disappearance and were also on the verge of losing all that they owned because of a stranger who turned up unexpectedly. They prayed for a miracle.

Contents

Chapter 1.
The Child from Hell

The lonely figure wearing a multi-coloured gypsy skirt walked slowly across the hot sands of the desert. The elderly lady's skirt was too long as she was only tiny, and her skirt wrapped itself around her ankles as she wandered to her tent.

She had not been able to sleep as she had an inkling that her nephew David and his wife Nat were having lots of problems with their little girl Katy, who was two years old.

Katy was the child from hell.

The last time Aunt Agatha had tuned into her family was at the birth of this toddler. David and Nat were unaware of her presence, but the baby could remember that there was someone special at the side of her crib and she cried inwardly wondering why this special person had abandoned her at such a young age. The newborn had wished that this presence would return one day. The baby was so scrawny and so vulnerable but had a dark halo around her which was not good. Agatha thought Katy had evil karma that needed releasing.

This baby needed help as she had a loneliness about her, and Aunt Agatha quickly sent out prayers for tiny Katy.

"Angels, please help this soul,
make her pretty make her whole.
Make her strong, make her nice,
fill her days with all things bright.
Take away her nasty side
or she will cause trouble and try to hide;
away from family, she will stray,
hating them more each day,
And will end up on her own, unhappy, sad and so alone."
"Please help her!" Agatha had prayed so hard.

Meanwhile, she snapped out of her past thoughts and came back to the present. As Agatha reached over for her bag of tricks, i.e., Tarot cards, crystal ball and a tattered ancient book on healing with herbs, the wind blew sand into the bag and she had to recover her belongings before they too were blown away.

Polishing the crystal ball till it was shining, she spoke to it ever so gently.

"Crystal ball round and bright, fill my body full of light.

Take me to the child within, help me rid her of all sin.

Help her know what is wrong from right and fill her soul with pure bright light."

Woooosh!

Agatha felt her tummy wobble as she was lifted into the realms of good magic and angels and all things wonderful.

She was on her way to make a visitation to young Katy who would not be aware of her.

As she was drawn down a tunnel of light, Agatha felt that her body was swirling around like some washing in a washing machine and she began to feel dizzy. Soon, the spinning slowed down allowing her to step into the young girl's space to do her good magic on the unsuspecting Katy who was lying in bed, her young mind full of menacing thoughts and plans.

Katy was restless and was tossing and turning in bed, trying to get comfortable. Her mop of golden blonde hair cascaded around her shoulders as she decided to focus on her fingers that were vibrating again; she was sick of it.

"Hmm, my fingers are burning again and tingling; what's going on?"

She was having this a lot lately, and, not wanting to say anything to her mum and dad, she decided to try and figure out what was causing it.

Staring at her fingers in the light of the moon shining through her bedroom curtains, she said out loud, "Can anyone help me? I know you are there". She sensed it again, the presence of someone in her room even though she could see no one. Suddenly, out of the shadows came a pink glow that energised the whole room.

Katy could feel a change in the atmosphere; it had a warm secure feel, and the young out-of-control little girl had only ever felt this emotion once. On the day she was born, it had entered her heart and it felt like it would burst, but something, or someone, was missing and she cried.

A column of beautiful dancing lights appeared before her and she had never experienced anything like this before.

"Well, this isn't real, I know," Katy mused. The child from hell did not trust anyone as she could not be trusted herself.

I must be dreaming again, she thought, but this time it was different, as she felt a lot of warmth in her heart as the array of lights engulfed the toddler and her bedroom.

The two-year-old tossed her unruly curly hair away from her face. "My dreams are normally about monsters and horrible things that I rather like," she chuckled deviously. "I am usually shown how to be very cruel and evil!"

She cackled with a blood-curdling noise that would frighten the devil out of his den. She suddenly sensed someone or something was there. "Oi! What are you hiding for?"

Patience was a virtue that Katy did not own. "Well, please yourself."

The glowing figure began to build up into a shimmering column of colours and danced across the room in front of the bewildered young blue-eyed girl who grabbed her book, and smack, smack - "Hm, missed it. Oi! Mr Invisible again, you make me sick; what are you playing at?" Katy was angry now.

Someone was speaking to her, well, whispering gently. "You have lots of special gifts, magic like, but only use them for good or you will suffer, pet. That's all I will say, for now, so use the light for love and good things in the world, little one." The voice faded. "Pet?! Pet! I am not a dog or a cat! What is that person talking about? Or is it a person? I cannot see anyone but it sounds like a lady." The young girl looked amused. "Special gifts, hmm? Well, we will see how special they are." Thoughts of mischief formed in Katy's nasty mind now. "Well, here goes." She was older than her years.

Jumping out of the bed, her duvet fell to the ground. Katy rushed to the window as the column of colour disappeared in front of her, leaving a trail of beautiful light dancing in the darkened room.

In the moonlight, she could see the old oak tree in the garden and it was gigantic. James, her brother, loved spending his spare time there on his swing and climbing up the stout branches to his treehouse as boys did.

"Mummy's boy, James," Katy snarled. She shrieked in excitement at her cruel plan.

Pointing her fingers that felt like they were on fire, she cried out:

"Special powers, do your thing, destroy the treehouse and the swing, tear the branches from the tree and kill its roots so all can see."

Katy's fingers were burning up and turned into long lasers of white light being fired like streaks of lightning, striking and destroying what she aimed at.

When her fingers were unbearably hot, she stopped and so did the power that she released. "I love it, I love it! I am in charge now!" She nearly wet herself with excitement as she saw the damage that she had done to James's special place. "Serves him right," she gloated. "I can't wait till James wakes up in the morning, as the big cry baby will have something to cry for!" She laughed as her mind was so full of tricks that she wanted to play pranks all the time. She had never looked so happy, as she enjoyed doing bad things, however, this evil streak of hers was going too far and could be dangerous.

Humming gently to herself, she crawled back into bed, tired out now with all the excitement, and dropped off to sleep with an evil smile on her face.

A sorry tiny figure surrounded by beautiful colours appeared to be crying pitifully as it faded away back to another part of the world.

"God, help Katy; I did warn her, but I guess this is the path that she has decided to take, silly child. I am so disappointed as I thought I could see some good in her the day she came into the world, but am I wrong?"

Agatha's family knew that she was on the other side of the world, however, they did not know that she had tuned her mind onto another wavelength through her crystal ball and was present at Katy's birth.

Aunt Agatha had used her crystal with all its magical properties and had zoomed into the young girl's world once again. She wrung her hands while crying, and was so disappointed at the special powers that were gifted to Katy, but which were, unfortunately, being used in such a destructive way.

I'm so sorry I made that visit to the unruly child, she thought. *I should never have given her the choice, but we all have free will and know right from wrong, so Katy will have to learn the hard way; it's called Karma. I will pray for her*. Agatha wept. "I will have to watch over the family to make sure no harm comes to them while I meditate on Katy's rebellious streak of anger and havoc," Agatha said, thinking out loud as she wearily reached her place of rest to contemplate on this young girl's future - if she had one. The tired aunt laid her head on her rolled-up blanket and she immediately fell into a deep sleep-like trance where her mind would step into another world of Sages and magic, a place where she would find the inspiration for bringing love into the heart of this two-year-old who was more like a teenager - a very rebellious teenager - with so much anger and hate; so sad. Aunt Agatha went into a meditative sleep, hoping to find answers.

The house groaned as the Bex family had awakened from their deep sleep and one by one, they got washed and dressed ready for breakfast. "Morning, Mum." James emptied some cornflakes into his cereal bowl, poured the milk on and scooped a spoonful greedily into his mouth. "Omg, what is this?" He was spitting it out onto the kitchen table.

"It's rabbit food, Mum, that stuff we feed Snowy with and it tastes foul. I bet she has been up to her old tricks again." James started to bang his fists on the table. "I will kill Katy, Mum, I swear; I hate her!" The eight-year-old was livid.

His face was red with anger, and he stormed outside to calm down, his brown eyes becoming dark with rage.

17

Mum, Nat, was fed up with it all and cried to their dad, "You will need to do something, David, or I will have a flipping breakdown." Their two-year-old daughter was becoming a nightmare and both parents were struggling to make her behave.

Katy had been listening to the commotion while hiding under the stairs near the kitchen. Her ears had pricked up on hearing Mum.

"Breakdown? What's she talking about? It's only cars that have breakdowns. Oh well, cart her off to the local garage; that will sort Mum out." She smirked at her own funny sense of humour.

Containing her laughter, Katy waited for James's reaction on going outside. She bit her hands hard to stop herself from chuckling as they would hear her. She loved her monstrous side and giggled.

James went round the back of the house to his favourite place to calm down but as he looked straight ahead, he was stunned at the destruction that had originally been a large beautiful oak tree. It was scattered all over the lawn, branches broken, the trunk was burned right through to the roots and his treehouse was no more.

His thick brown hair was soaked with the rain that was now pouring down on the wreckage in the garden, but he had not heard any thunder or lightning which would probably have been the cause of the damage. Strange! He was deep in thought now.

He screamed as he ran back into the house, shocked to the core.

Katy tried to make a speedy exit as James dashed through the front door, but it wound up that her brother was too quick for her, and, as she tried to climb up the stairs, he grabbed her nightdress, pulling her down the last three stairs, bump, bump, bump. "Ow! That flipping hurt!" Katy cried.

"Get off me, you muppet!" Katy kicked out at her red-faced brother, the pupils in his brown eyes like black coals as he tried to punch her. "You evil brat! I hate you!" James was furious.

Katy felt smug. She had won again and caused havoc in the home.

"I will make you eat Snowy's food and see how you like it." He shook her.

Dad stepped in and split them up, taking Katy's hand firmly in his massive shovel-like hands.

"Well, madam, grounded again. When are you going to learn?" Shaking his head, David shouted, "Get back to your room; you are grounded for a week". He was so angry.

"Dad, did you hear the thunder and lightning last night?" James asked, still in a state of shock at seeing his treehouse destroyed beyond recognition.

David scratched his head as he looked at Nat, his wife, then asked, "What thunder and lightning? There wasn't any unless we slept so well that we missed it. Did you hear it, Nat?" "No, David, not a thing."

"Well, come out and see the oak tree, Dad." James was still upset.

David was horrified when he saw the destruction and knew who was responsible for the chaos - Katy! She must be the child from hell.; she was evil, and he was worried about what she would do next.

"Grounded again!! I don't care, I have special magic now so it will not bother me." Katy smiled to herself as they did not know of the powers she had just been introduced to, even though she had a choice of using them for good.

"Good is boring so why not cause suffering to this blinking family who don't even like me?" She giggled to herself even though she was in for a long, lonely day.

Throwing herself onto her bed, she chuckled as her mind was planning her next fiasco for the next unlucky victim.

David walked back into the kitchen slowly wondering what to do for the best. "Stick the kettle on, James, and we will try to sort this out."

"It will not fit me, Dad." James had calmed down now and Dad pretended to give James a clout round the ear but grinned as he knew his boy would soon bounce back.

As they sat around the kitchen table, eleven-year-old Dione appeared. "What is all the noise about? No, that is a silly question. Is witchy poo up to her old tricks as usual?"

"Yes!" they said in unison.

After tying her long brown hair into a ponytail, she sat down and sipped her cup of tea while James explained what had gone on with Katy, his breakfast, and the loss of his precious treehouse.

None of them were aware of what danger their younger sister could put them all in.

"Don't you think you should take Katy to see the doctor?" She felt she had to make Mum and Dad realise that the evil antics of her younger sister had gone on long enough now.

Eleven-year-old Dione had always been a sensible child and was called goody two shoes by Katy, however, she worried about her little sister's behaviour as it was becoming more daring.

Chapter 2.
Football Fiasco

Meanwhile, Katy's mind was working overtime at the chaos she was going to create very shortly.

Rubbing her hands together, she screeched out, "I wonder how big sister will feel after I have sorted her out. She never puts a foot wrong; they should have called her Snow White!" Combing her golden blonde hair, she began to hatch a plan to annoy her brother again.

Looking in the mirror, Katy's eyes began to change colour from blue to green as they sparkled with mischief and she thought about her family whom she disliked knowing they would all be calling her.

Her family sat talking amongst themselves. It was Sunday so no rushing about for school or work until tomorrow, however, David reminded his son that he had football tomorrow and not to forget to clean his boots again after having a game of footie in the garden. "I won't, Dad. You know how much I love football." David was so very proud of his son and smiled. "Yes, Dad, and we have the finals tomorrow with Buxton Juniors, but I am sure we will win. After all, I am the best player that the school has, and you will agree, Dad, of course, but you know that already." His eyes shone with pride as he went to clean his boots. I will knit you a big hat for your big head," Dione replied jokingly.

Katy liked being on her own as she liked creating her next evil move. "At least the family will notice me then. I will not tell them about my special powers yet, but let them all sweat a bit, as I am not finished with James yet.

I will let it come as a shock, lol, and shock it will be if I use my laser fingers! Bahahaha!" Her cackle echoed through the house.

Katy was deep in thought now planning her next move and as her mind was spinning out of control, a voice whispered gently in her ear which startled her.

"I was there the day you were born, you looked alone and so forlorn, pink and wrinkled no hair at all, you were frail and so small.

But I cast a spell or two, make her pretty that will do but I did not realise, you were born a horrible child.

I came to help you bringing light, to guide you and make you aware of what's right.

I cannot help you anymore, till I come knocking at your door.

So, little child, heed what I say, or you will end up lost one day.

No one to love or care for you, but I will help if you try too, so, think upon these words, my dear, until the day when I appear."

Aunt Agatha backed away slowly from Katy. "Night, night and God bless." Agatha was so sad, but soon she found herself back in her own bed.

She prayed that night for Katy.

Katy crept down the stairs ever so quietly as she knew the family were all in bed now but may still be awake.

"I must take my time for if Dad hears me, well, goodness knows what he will do next. He will probably have a heart attack, the colour he was turning earlier, stupid man."

As she made her way downstairs and into the bathroom, Katy hoped she would find James's precious football boots.

"Yes!" she said and nearly clapped her hands. "Silly me, nearly gave the game away."

James had cleaned his boots and set them on a shelf above the radiator so they would dry overnight.

As Katy reached up for the boots, she wondered how to carry out her nasty deed. *Hmm, I will need some help here,* she thought to herself.

The football boots were nearly new and were James's pride and joy as they were not cheap ones. He had helped Mum to buy them by saving up his pocket money.

Katy started chanting and the atmosphere became electric.

"Think he will win the game today?

Not with my magic powers, no way!

Shrink his boots from heel to toe;

Man of the match? I do not think so."

Suddenly, the boots were yanked out of Katy's hands by an invisible force and dropped into the toilet. The water rapidly swirled around them tossing them up and down in the bowl. It looked as if they were in a washing machine.

"Ha! I love it."

Katy went back to her room without making any noise as she floated up the stairs effortlessly.

"It is the power I have." Katy opened her bedroom door and climbed into bed, very satisfied at what she had achieved.

Studying her fingers, the next plot was building up in her mind as she pulled the duvet up under her chin.

The child from hell was asleep with the evil smile on her mouth that seemed to be getting wider and wider.

Morning soon came around and Katy was so looking forward to the outcome as the day unfolded.

After they all had breakfast and James made sure his was not rabbit food, he went to retrieve his 'footie boots' as he called them from the downstairs bathroom.

"Oh no! I don't believe it!" James was devastated at seeing first his laces hanging over the side of the toilet, and then his boots, inside the toilet bowl, full of water.

"They must have fallen off the shelf. I should have been more careful. Oh well, I am sure I can still play my best with damp boots on."

He grabbed a towel and began to rub them dry.

"What is the commotion about, James? I could hear you from outside."

"C'mon, you two, I will be late for work by the time I drop you all off at school."

"Moan, moan, blooming moan." Katy looked at her father who was becoming irritable now.

"What did you say, young lady?" David was near boiling point.

"Nuffin, Dad, I said nuffin," Katy replied with a sickly smile. "Get back in the house with Mum and behave yourself or you will have me to contend with," David yelled. "Ok, whatever," Katy whispered as she went back indoors to spend the boring day.

Grinning like a Cheshire cat, Katy knew Dad was becoming more irritable at her behaviour, especially when he yelled.

"You mean nothing, young lady, nothing! Do you hear me?"

"No, she has got cloth ears, Dad." James doubled up with laughter. David was not amused and scowled; he was fed up with Katy; her tantrums and bad behaviour were getting to him and he'd had enough.

As Katy went into the house with Mum, she stuck her tongue out at Dad as he drove away in a world of his own, fuming at his child from hell.

Learning how to read, write, memorise the alphabet and arithmetic was so boring, thought Katy, even though she was a clever two-year-old. "Why does Mum not buy me a smartphone? The other two have got one, but no, not me." She sat down at the kitchen table imagining what would be going on at the football match at James's school.

"Wish I was a fly on the goalpost," she giggled to herself.

The Buxton boys' football team were getting changed into their football strip as James and the rest of his team joined them in the dressing room of Grange School, the school that James had been going to since he was five years old and he loved it. He was the most popular boy in his class and was very academic as Nat had taught him and Dione in their early years before starting school.

You name it, he was the best, especially at football, which he excelled at, and he was the captain of the team.

A voice boomed out; "Are you lads ready yet? You are taking long enough. Stop the talking and get walking." It was the football coach, Mr Maverick.

The lads made their way to the football field and eventually the game started. As the whistle was blown, the boys were in good fighting spirit as they all wanted their team to win, of course.

They kicked, headed and tackled as they moved the ball up and down the field trying to get a goal in first.

The game progressed for about twenty minutes and James felt that his boots were drying out as they were getting tighter. The ball was passed to him and he saw his chance.

He lined the ball up and was taking a goal kick when he missed.

"What?! I have never, ever missed a goal kick." Blushing, James went as red as the stripe on his football strip when the other team started laughing at him.

"Got that wrong, didn't you, smarty-pants?" one of his rivals from the other team jeered, as James started to dance on the pitch like a ballet dancer. The more he tried to control his feet, the more they took on a life of their own. The Buxton boys were in tears laughing.

I will show them, thought James, but as he ran forward into a tackle, he felt that his feet were being strangled. His legs started to turn a grey colour and his boots were becoming tighter and tighter. They were shrinking before his eyes.

"Player of the year, that's a laugh!" the rival footballer rubbed it in while goading James who was in real trouble now.

He fell to the ground as many of the other team players were now taking the mickey out of him.

"The man of the match, he has gone down like a ballerina prancing around."

They were really taunting him now, jeering and annoying him also.

The Buxton lads rolled all over the pitch, laughing their heads off as James hobbled off part of the way and then collapsed. He knew Evil Katy had something to do with this; he just knew it.

He cried when he went into the dressing room as he had been embarrassed by the boys' taunts and worst of all, by letting his own team down.

He would have to calm down before he got home, or there would be murder at the Bex family home, as he was ready to kill his younger sister yet again. He imagined getting her and throttling her. "I hate her!" he cried.

It was a big operation getting the boots off James's feet but such a relief as the colour came flowing back to his legs and his sore feet.

The teacher had to cut James's expensive boots off his feet; they were ruined, and James was devastated. It was his worst day ever.

He could not wait to get back home as he felt so ashamed and was glad when Dad arrived to pick him up.

"Dad, it was awful. I felt that my feet were the size of a baby's and my legs were so swollen they looked massive. I will never live this down, ever." David felt so sorry for his son and tried to comfort him.

"Well, it's not the end of the world, you know, son.

I will get to the bottom of this if it kills me," he promised James.

Dione hugged James after he calmed down and thought about her sister becoming more out of control than ever.

Something was obviously wrong with Katy – it was obvious after the prank that she had played on nine-year-old James, who was in a state of shock.

Must make Mum take her to the doctor's straight away.

Dione was deep in thought as to what problem Katy could have. She gazed out of the car window as they arrived home.

Sitting around the table, the story of James's nightmare slowly began to unfold.

"I won't be able to live this down ever, Mum, and I was supposed to be the best player ever." He was devastated and sobbed uncontrollably.

"Now, now, what son of mine gives up so easily, James? Not you, I know." David winked at Nat, his wife, who felt sorry for James.

"Children soon forget. It will be a seven-day wonder and we will make sure that Monster Mash does not try any more of her sadistic tricks if it is her fault."

Although David had no proof it was Katy's doing, he just knew.

"Doctor's tomorrow, Nat. We will find out what's going on once and for all."

Meanwhile, Katy, who was listening in from the window in the back garden, had to stifle her hysterical witch-like cackle.

"Monster Mash? Flipping Monster Mash! I will show them what I am capable of, with my wonderful monstrous magical gift." She scooted down the garden and eyed up the bonfire with its stacks of wood overflowing. James and his friends had spent weeks collecting and building it all up and there was still stuff to go on it from the shed that needed clearing out.

Katy's mind was in overdrive.

"Are you out there, Katy? Your tea is ready." Nat had sent Dione out to find the horror and decided not to mention about James's disaster but wait till they got Katy to the doctor's the following day.

Nat was not looking forward to this one bit.

"Why am I going to the doctor's, then?" Katy knew why but acted dumb as she knew how to act in front of Doctor Wood. She was so crafty.

After a ten-minute drive, they arrived at the medical centre.

"Hi Mrs Bex, Mr Bex." The Doctor was a very jovial man and made them feel relaxed in his company. Straightening his spectacles, he leaned forward. "Now then, what's the problem?"

Nat and David explained that Katy's bad behaviour was becoming serious, and that they were really concerned at how far she would go with her pranks.

After speaking to the two-year-old, who came over as sweet as an angel, the Doctor took note of her general health and retorted, "ADHD - that's her problem. You need to change her diet. No fizzy drinks, no sweets and certainly no junk food, that's all. Nothing to worry about as lots of children have it. You are not on your own, and I am sure you can deal with it." Smiling, the Doctor said goodbye to the parents who looked shell-shocked.

When they got outside and into the car, they were both stunned at the doctor's statement but knew they had to try and curb Katy's bad behaviour, starting with her diet, of course, which they both knew would not go down well with their uncontrollable daughter.

She will end up ruling us if she carries on this way and I am not prepared to let that happen, thought David.

Reading her dad's thoughts, Katy smirked. "We will see, won't we? But I will not be giving in just like that."

Her eyes danced with devilment as she stubbornly folded her arms tightly and grimaced. "Well, just wait and see." Katy closed her eyes, planning her next escapade with a vengeance. "Monster Mash, indeed; they will all be sorry."

Chapter 3.
Fury and Fire

The following day, Nat decided to start with the special diet for Katy of toast for breakfast as no sugary cereals were allowed.

"I am not eating this crap." Katy threw the toast across the kitchen floor as Nat looked on, flabbergasted.

"Who do you think you are talking to and how dare you use words like that in this house? Do you hear me?!" Mum felt like smacking her.

"Talk to the hand as the face isn't listening." Katy had put her hand in front of her face between her and her mother.

"Get out, get out, you little evil person! I am finding this all too much. Wait till your dad comes home."

"Whatever." Katy's behaviour was shocking as she flounced out of the kitchen and up the stairs.

She made her way into her mother's bedroom with revenge in her heart and glanced around.

She quickly rummaged through her Mum's wardrobe, dragging clothes out and throwing them out of the window. She then grabbed a couple of pairs of shoes that were Nat's new ones and they followed out of the window.

Good job Mum's room is at the front of the house away from the kitchen, Katy thought, grinning from ear to ear.

She made her way downstairs and out of the front door without being seen.

Picking the heap of her mother's clothes and shoes up in her arms, bit by bit, she threw them on the bonfire.

Now for something out of Dad's shed! Her mind was ticking over rapidly.

There was an old tin and bits and bobs, not much, she thought, but that would do for now as the other shed was in view of the kitchen, and they might see what she was up to.

She kicked Topsy the cat on the way back upstairs, and it screeched as it ran as far away from her as possible. Topsy knew what this little girl was capable of after it had spent time in the washer till Nat had rescued it.

"Mum, have you seen my laptop? I left it on the table in the lounge."

Dione had spent all evening swatting up on information for some exams and had made a lot of important notes on what she had learned so far about veterinary practices.

"Sorry, Dione, I haven't seen it." Then together, they both said, "Oh no! Katy!" They both ran upstairs as Katy had been grounded after tea and sent to her bedroom.

They barged into her room but there was no sign of her.

"OMG, where has she gone this time?"

They raced downstairs wondering what they might find… or not find, as the case may be.

Katy had found a lighter in her dad's old shed and had waited till it had gone dark to do as much damage as she could to all the family. "Hurt them like they hurt me."

She really enjoyed slinging goody two shoes' laptop on the bonfire along with nasty Mum's clothes. Ha. Ha. She was becoming madder by the minute.

As Nat and Dione stepped outside, they were appalled at what they saw.

Katy had a malicious grin on her face, but worst of all, she had flicked the lighter on and had lit the bottom of the pile of wood ready for bonfire night.

"NO!!" cried Nat as she noticed a petrol can from Dad's old shed on the fire.

Too late! Woosh! The whole lot went up, exploding like a bomb as it spread onto David's shed and onto the thatched roof of their cottage.

"KATY!" Mum screamed hysterically as she managed to drag her child away from the blazing fire, getting burns on her own hands as she did so.

Dione cried at the loss of all the work on her laptop, which was gone now, but ran indoors for Dad.

"Fire brigade, urgent, as house on fire. Hurry up, please." There was urgency in his voice as the fire had spread into the home itself.

By the time the fire engine turned up, the house was like a bombsite with only part of the cottage left. It would need lots of money spent on it, as it had lots of smoke damage.

Katy was trembling and did not hear Mum say, "David, we have not paid the house insurance since you went on shorter hours at work."

They both sobbed as the three children stood back looking on with faces blackened from the smoke. David saw the worry on Nat's face and reassured her.

"I will get extra work and we will get through this, so do not worry."

David tried to convince Nat, but her mind was on her young daughter. *We could all have died*, she thought as a cold shiver ran through her. *We would have been burnt to a crisp*.

Katy read her mother's mind and chuckled as she imagined them all in packets on a shelf in the local shop.

"Burnt to a crisp, yeh. I would be salt and vinegar, James is cheesy so cheese and onion. Dione is plain and I think Mum and Dad could have been Barbecue, lol!" She was in fits of laughter now with tears rolling down her cheeks as she held her tummy which was sore from her evil laughter.

Another good day for me, thought Katy.

She went looking for Topsy the kitten who was hiding in the rabbit hutch with Snowy, the beautiful white rabbit, hence the name.

"Hmm, good job you were not on the bonfire." She glared at the timid animals as they backed off gently out of her reach. The vulnerable pair huddled close together. They were so frightened of what Katy might do next as they had both been mistreated in the past many times by this monster of a child. They kept as still as statues and eventually both fell asleep due to the hypnotic stare that emanated from the strange little girl.

"What is the matter with her, Dione? I am sick to the back teeth of her crying all day and night; I don't know what to do anymore."

Natalie was tired out with it all as Katy looked at her through pretend tears and said, "Are you sick of me to the front teeth as well? Hahaha!" Nat was not amused and went to prepare supper for David who was due in from working a twelve-hour shift. "Shower and bedtime, children." Mum wanted the children settled and asleep before David came home as he had been so tired for weeks now.

"It is getting late and well past your bedtime, little one."

After they had a shower and their hair was dry, Katy started crying as Dione helped her upstairs.

Monster kicked and screamed as Dione tried to settle her in bed.

"I want to sleep in Mum's bed as me having bad dreams!" she cried.

"Why, am I not surprised." Dione glared at her unruly little sister. "It is because you are a horrible little person."

"SHUT UP!" The horrible little person lashed out at Dione who felt a sharp pain in her tummy from Katy's kicking. Shouting for Mum to come and sort out her brat of a sister, Dione lay down with her knees pulled up to alleviate the discomfort, knowing it would wear off soon.

As David walked through the door, Nat noticed how tired he looked after working a twelve-hour shift and she gave him a big hug while ignoring Katy's crying.

"C'mon, have some supper then up to bed. You looked tired."

"Yes, but I will be ok, Nat." He wondered how long he could carry on working these longer hours as it had been three months since the horrible fire, and they had to find money for repairs and then Christmas on top of it all. It was never-ending.

He ate his food in silence then nodded to Nat that he was ready for his bed and made his way up the stairs.

No sooner had he got into bed when Katy started screaming her head off, again and again, knowing that eventually, they would let her share their bed.

No sleep for me, David thought as he climbed into bed and Nat joined him with screaming Katy in her arms.

They settled down to sleep and the smirk on Katy's face began to grow bigger and bigger. "HAH! Got my own way again."

Chapter 4.
Unexpected Visitor

Bang, bang! What a racket as the noise echoed through the house.

"Who the heck is that at this time in the morning?" David grumbled as he jumped out of the double bed which looked as if a tornado had hit it, thanks to Katy tossing and turning all night in between screaming.

Nat and David were both worn out as it had taken nearly all night to eventually settle her down.

"I don't believe it." Nat was fuming as her child from hell started screaming again.

"There is someone at the front door, David."
"Tell me something I don't know, Nat."
David was struggling to put his slippers on.

He jumped down the stairs, two at a time and wondered who it could be at five in the morning.

Knock, knock, knock! It sounded like someone was taking the door off its hinges.

"Hang on a minute, will you? I'm coming." David was furious by this time, as he was so tired, and he'd had no sleep.

Unlocking the door, David stood back cautiously and struggled to see who it was, as there was only the brightness from the moon shining on this tiny figure who stood there.

"Put the light on, that's a good lad, and come and give yer old aunt a big hug."

David stepped forward to have a closer look at the unexpected visitor.

"It can't be… oh, flippin' 'eck, it is, it's Aunt Agatha! Where have you been hiding yourself all these years?" David was so shocked but in a nice way.

"Don't just stand there wi' yer gob open, gimme a hug and let me in."

The old lady was cold, wet, weary and awfully hungry, but not necessarily in that order.

She was born in Byker Grove, Newcastle upon Tyne in England over sixty-five years ago but still had the strong Geordie accent that originated from that area, and each word spoken sounded as if it was being sung.

It was certainly music to David's ears as he helped his aunt remove her soaking wet coat.

"I could have picked a better night than this, rain, hail and thunder; all we need now is snow." Agatha's teeth chattered with the cold as she entered their abode.

"Eee, it's lovely and warm in here, pet." She smiled and thought how fortunate she was at being here among relatives who loved her. She suddenly had a wonderful feeling of contentment in her heart.

"Nat, Nat! Can you guess who is here?"

"He asks some stupid questions at this time in the morning," mumbled Nat to herself as she tried to pacify Katy whose face was blue through holding her breath while screaming. Also, her unruly hair was all over her face, soaking wet with her false tears.

Patience - that's what I need, patience, and a good night's sleep, Nat thought as she slowly came down the stairs trying to hide her anger at this time in the morning. On reaching the hallway, Nat was aware of a warm presence that seemed to envelop the immediate surroundings. This made her curious.

"Nat, this is my Aunt Agatha who I thought I would never see again."

David was so proud to introduce these two lovely people to each other and as tears came to his eyes, he quickly wiped them away as he did not want them to know how sensitive he was.

"Pleased to meet you, pet, very pleased to meet you." Aunt Agatha greeted Nat warmly and held her hand in hers, feeling an instant bond between them.

"You look tired, just like a bombed-out earwig. Here, let me take the tot off you." Aunt Agatha leaned forward eager to take the child to comfort her, noticing her red tear-stained face and her unruly hair that needed tying back.

Nat was a bit reluctant to pass the distraught child to Aunt Agatha, declining quickly as the toddler stretched her chubby arms out to the lovely old lady.

"C'mon, sweetheart. What are all your tears for? You will break someone's heart one day - perhaps mine?" Agatha felt that special connection with Katy as on the day the child was born, a day she would unfortunately never forget.

The insecure Katy's tears and tantrums stopped immediately, as she was mesmerised by the magical presence of this old lady, rosy-cheeked, happy and with a beautiful smile.

Katy was puzzled by the shining blue stars that were dancing around Aunt Agatha's head and deep down, she felt a stirring of love deep within her heart.

Something mystical was happening as Katy's heart filled with love and she could sense that a new way of life was about to begin.

Katy felt the warmth and the chubbiness of Aunt Agatha as she laid her head on her bosom.

She cuddled in further until she imagined that she was being protected by a warm cosy duvet.

It was a different world in here, her mind told her, and to Mum and Dad's amazement, Katy nodded off with a contented smile on her tiny angelic face.

"Well, wonders will never cease!" They smiled at each other and sighed.

"I knew you would come, my special person." Katy snuggled in deeper and deeper, the love from her aunt enfolding her like a warm ray of sunshine.

"Thanks, Aunt Agatha."

Within a day of her arrival, the whole house had taken on a wonderful feeling of peace.

The whole household adored Agatha and after a couple of weeks, Nat approached her nervously.

"It's heaven, Aunt Agatha, and David and I." Nat stammered.

"Let me stop you there, pet. Call me Agatha; it saves time, and it is a bit of a mouthful, ok? Now, as you were saying, Nat?"

Her aunt wrapped her arms around this sweet girl she had come to love.

"David and I have been doing a lot of talking, and we both feel that you fit into our lives like a glove, and we want you to think about staying permanently. Will you, pleeease?"

Nat was begging Agatha as she crossed her fingers behind her back.

"We haven't got much money, as you know, but we do have lots of love for you."

"Hmm. I didn't believe that I should be that lucky, my dear, and after such a short time of me arriving here."

Agatha knew her dream was coming true.

"I have also had a lot to think about of late and I think it's time that I sat down and told you both what's been going on in my life."

"As you already know, I have been a charity worker in Africa for the last fifteen years, and while I was there, I also learned a lot about herbal remedies and astrology. As I learned these, I also developed strong psychic powers that enabled me to help people when they came to me with their problems or aches and pains that were eased with herbs and special healings.

"These skills, or gifts as I call them, were passed down to me by a great African Sage or you may call him a Wiseman of the village. Anyway, I am going off the most important part of this incredible story." Aunt Agatha was becoming extremely excited now, as she got comfortable on the old chunky cream settee and began plumping up the cushions behind her.

"Are you listening, children? Well, I shall begin." They laughed.

"Yes, we are all ears - well, nobody's perfect." David was intrigued by his aunt's tale up to now.

"Remember that good friend of mine, David, Wendy Hibbert from the Vicarage in Glossop?"

David could not remember; however, he just went along with his elderly aunt.

"Course I can." He blushed as he coughed. "Yes, yes."

"Well, Wendy's parents died many years ago, and as you know, she was an only child."

Where is all this leading to? thought David as he twitched nervously, scratching his ear. *Hold your horses, David, be patient.* He squirmed nervously in his seat.

Agatha was becoming more excited now at the news she was about to share.

God, she knows what I am thinking! Better watch my Ps and Qs! David apologised. "Sorry."

"John Knox solicitors from Higham contacted me while I was in Africa; I am surprised that they tracked me down.

However, spirits work in mysterious ways."

Agatha noticed how enthralled these two lovely people were and wondered what response she would eventually get from them when she finally gave them all the good news.

"I cannot wait to see their happy faces." Her eyes shone.

"As Wendy had no living relatives, she made out her will leaving all her worldly goods to me."

"What have you inherited?" Nat could have kicked herself for being so tactless.

Agatha leaned towards the couple. "What have WE inherited! I say 'we' as I want you all to share in my good fortune. We have two million pounds and a great big manor house in the country. Please say you will be my new family as I would rattle around in a house of its size on my own. So, how about it, you two lovebirds?"

Nat gazed at David with a wistful look and knew what their answer would be.

"We will have to put it to Dione and James as they will have to change school."

David was shocked and happy at the same time with this good news, but his head was buzzing as he had not taken it all in - it seemed too good to be true.

On telling the children, they were delighted at their response.

"Wheeeee, great, and my own bedroom, that will do for me!" shouted James, who was jumping all over the place like a jack in the box with excitement.

Dione was also so pleased with not having to share as, since the fire, the three children had been sleeping in one bedroom.

"Great! That means that brother of mine won't mess with my tablet and Monster Mash won't keep destroying my clothes. Hope I make new friends and then they can have a sleepover." Dione was a quiet girl and did not make friends very easily, however, a new home might make all the difference as she had felt so upset and embarrassed when their home was nearly destroyed, and kids at school were taking the mickey like kids do.

Aunt Agatha had a brilliant bond with the children, and it was plain to see that they would all be happy living together, especially in a home where Agatha would have her own bedroom instead of a fold-up sofa-bed in the lounge. Not that she complained, as she was happy to be back with family and it showed.

When they all retired for the night, Nat and David, who were dumbstruck with the good news, had lots to talk about.

All their personal belongings would have to be packed.

They decided to get all the family involved with the packing, except for one little person who now never left her aunt's side.

The couple were over the moon at the change in their child from hell, who had become an angel overnight.

"We have got lots of things to sort out to take with us, so Dione and James, I am sure you are both capable of packing up your belongings." Nat was so excited - the sooner they moved the better, and that's why she asked the children to muck in. She left them in control of their own personal stuff.

"James, start bundling up your Xbox games because the sooner we get everything sorted, the sooner we can move to our lovely big home," muttered Dione.

James had lots of games that he had collected over the past few years and he was careful when packing them as he loved all his games.

Meanwhile, Dione was picking out the clothes she wanted, and the older ones that were too small for her, would go to the local charity shop in Ashfield.

Their home was sold at a loss, but it did not matter as they were off on a new adventure without the worry of money and, most of all, without the worry of Katy, who had become so well behaved since Aunt Agatha arrived. *How long will it last?* Nat asked herself, not building her hopes up.

They hired a removal van for the bits and pieces that they had decided to take with them. It was mostly personal stuff, clothes, games, pots and pans, dishes and garden tools.

They were going to replace beds, bedding, sofas and carpets etc., with new, as they were ruined with smoke when they had that big bonfire. They could laugh about it now but at the time it was horrendous.

Chapter 5.
Maple Manor and Angel's Den

"Dad! Dad! The furniture van is here!" James was buzzing as he skipped down the path as the blue removals van pulled up beside their once beautiful house, but that was history now as they had a great future ahead of them.

Two strapping lads made their way to the front door.

"Are we at the right house?" the big guy said abruptly, as he squinted at the fresh-faced boy who was happily swinging on the gate.

"Yes, of course it is. Can't you see the boxes piled up here on our doorstep?"

"Cheeky blighter." The younger man pretended to clout James, who ducked down just in case he was serious.

The van was soon stacked up with all their belongings and the family were going to follow in David's new car that his big-hearted aunt had gifted to him; it was his pride and joy.

Aunt Agatha held Katy's hand as the now three-year-old clutched onto her tightly with a look of fear in her bright blue eyes.

"Whatever is the matter with you, pet?" The loving maternal lady had been keen to have Katy sit next to her as something was worrying Aunt Agatha. She was concerned as her little niece had been acting strangely for weeks now; it was as if she did not want to move home.

"Nothing, Aunt Agatha." The child smiled sweetly. How could she tell the lovely elderly lady of the unforeseen circumstances that only she sensed would happen in the future?

The blonde haired child knew that she had to make the most of the time she had with her beloved aunt, as their time together would be short. She just knew it.

Katy wiped a tear from her eye and held tightly onto her aunt's hand, not knowing that she was part of the reason why Aunt Agatha had come back to David and his family, to help their unruly child take the right path of goodness, not evil. Aunt Agatha had seen a big difference in her young niece's behaviour immediately and hoped it would stay like that.

On and on the furniture van drove, winding its way up hill and down dale. The scenery was breath-taking, and the family were in awe of the wonderful views that were all around them.

Katy was growing up fast without knowing.

"There are a lot of farms between the lovely green fields," she said.

Katy's statement was very astute for the three-year-old, but she was an old soul and was not aware of it.

She had been on this earth before, not that she remembered, but Aunt Agatha did.

"And it's miles away from the noisy towns," said Dione, who liked the feeling of peace and stillness that she sensed above the noise of the car engine.

"There are lots of horses." It was part of Dione's nature to love animals and that's why she wanted to become a vet. She was in her element as there were many different species of animals out in the country.

The people carrier that Aunt Agatha had bought David was well worth the money as they were able to travel in comfort with plenty of room for them all.

"Good old Aunt Agatha!" James shouted loudly. "Hip, hip, hooray!" All the family clapped as they agreed.

"Enough of the old," said Agatha, then she thanked them. She was looking forward to reaching their destination; for a start, she was hungry and dying for a cup of tea.

The removal van had done many miles, and as they passed through a small village called Higham, the driver knew that the journey was nearing its end.

"Thank God we are nearly there, Jack," he mumbled to the younger man who was nodding off to sleep with boredom.

David's passengers all strained their necks to see what was ahead of them. Up an uneven very long and pebbly path the car bounced and weaved until they came across an opening in the many trees that surrounded them.

Were they here? Had they arrived at their destination?

They looked at each other in excitement mixed with fear of the unknown. They were apprehensive of what loomed ahead and Katy wanted a wee now but kept quiet. *It won't be long now; I can feel it in my water, hee, hee.* She sat silent, deep in thought.

"Wow, look at that," Katy exclaimed, her eyes shining brightly.

There, in all its glory, stood a magnificent mansion built in Derbyshire stone, pale grey rough blocks of beautiful stone with five windows to the front of the property and a sturdy brown oak front door in the centre.

Maple Manor certainly lived up to its name as the long drive up to the house was edged with maple trees on either side of the pathway. They stood like tin soldiers guarding the wonderful mansion.

"C'mon, hurry up, Dione." James could not get out of the car quickly enough and David grumbled, "Don't move from your seats till the car stops as it's dangerous." Dad had noticed that his son had taken his seat belt off in anticipation of jumping out.

"Sorry, Dad, you are right," agreed James, as he waited impatiently for the car to come to a halt.

"James, James, I want to come too." Katy struggled out of Aunt Agatha's arms, and, jumping out of the car, ran after her older brother. The children were so excited that they were running all over the place, not knowing which way to go.

They explored the gardens, which were magical, with a wooden bridge spanning across the cool water of the small stream filled with fish, and lots of wildlife too. The children eventually came to the front of the house knowing that the door would be unlocked, and they could go back to the garden later.

"Ye gads!" gasped Aunt Agatha. The elderly aunt was amazed at the size of the spacious hallway, which was square, with a long stairway running up the centre of the back wall, and dividing at the top, one landing on the left, the other to the right, with bedrooms off both.

Aunt Agatha had employed interior decorators prior to them moving in, and they had done an excellent job of the decorating, laying carpets and placing furniture. The floor of the hall was inlaid with highly polished oak floorboards partially covered by a plush Indian carpet in rich colours of reds, greens and rusts. It all looked very posh.

What a welcoming sight.

"Time to choose our bedrooms, don't you think, little one?" Her niece looked at her aunt lovingly and smiled.

"Yes, please."

Nat held David's hand tenderly as the kids bounded in, pushing past them as this was like an adventure to them; a wonderful dream come true.

Katy was hanging back from all the joviality as she knew that this happiness would not last - for her at least. She sobbed inwardly as Aunt Agatha held her hand and walked up the long stairway that was covered in a red carpet. *So warm to look at,* thought the elderly lady.

There were five bedrooms and a smaller room which was at the very end of the long landing-like corridor on the right.

Katy knew as soon as she saw the small room that it had magical qualities with the arch-shaped window which was beautifully inlaid with coloured glass and the figure of an angel in blue and white robes with golden gossamer wings.

It was awesome. Katy sensed that this room was going to play a special part in her future. *I don't know what, but I can feel it in my bones,* she thought. A cold shiver flowed down her spine.

"Well, well, well, what have we got here then, pet?" Aunt Agatha fell in love with this tiny room straight away. Her intuition told her it was the right place to do her special work in.

"Angel's Den that's what I will call it, Angel's Den. This room was made for me, Nat; all I ask is that I can claim it for my sanctuary."

There was no denying her aunt this space, as it was a small price to pay. After all, it was through Agatha's generosity that they were here.

"I bagsy this room." James had chosen one of the rooms which looked out onto the back gardens and he had a great view of the small river that was every boy's dream. Dione chose one at the other side of the landing from James, peace and quiet to study. *Just what I need, she thought.* The beautiful young lady was happy.

"Can I sleep in the same room as Aunt Agatha?" Katy piped up. "Pleeeaase?"

"No, I don't think that would be fair on Aunt Agatha, but you can have the room next door. Will that suit you?" David waited for some response from his youngest daughter. "Well, I suppose so, Dad." Katy seemed happier now.

Wonders will never cease, David mused. *That was easier than I thought.* "Now to sort Mum and Dads," he laughed, as that was not difficult. There was only one room left, overlooking the beautiful orchard at the back of the house.

Dione's room was opposite James's, as far away as possible, which would allow her all the quietness she needed.

Everyone was happy and later, the adult put their feet up, and enjoyed a well-earned cup of coffee and some cream doughnuts.

It had been a long day, but ever such a good day.

Aunt Agatha had lots of plans for Angel's Den and could not wait to put them into action.

"One step at a time now, Agatha, take your time," she whispered to herself as her mind began to unfold, tumbling with new ideas.

Katy was in her element with Aunt Agatha to turn to for love and guidance, and when Aunt asked for a family meeting, the young girl knew that her life was going to change. She was so excited but there was a cloud of sadness hanging over her that she could not shake off. She was so bewildered and felt lost in that moment.

Everyone gathered in the lounge eager to find out what Aunt Agatha had to say to them.

"Right, are you all listening?" Aunt Agatha's voice was quiet but firm. "I have lots of ideas going round in my head and would like to share them with you so that you can give me your opinions on them, so don't be frightened to speak up, ok?"

They all listened eagerly as they knew that Aunt Agatha's plans would be special and that she always had the family's welfare at heart.

"David, I know you will be back at work next week, back to normal hours, but if you want to give up work that's up to you."

"Never! It would drive me mad being at home all day," he laughed.

"It's Nat who wants a part-time job, isn't it, Nat?" David glanced towards Nat who looked so embarrassed but wanted to be back at work. She stuttered, "W-well, y-yes."

"I was coming to that," said Aunt Agatha quickly.

"I know you need your mind stimulating, Nat, so, the council are advertising office vacancies, and I can see the kids off to school and babysit Katy for you. However, I also have some plans for myself if you all agree on them?" She watched their faces in anticipation of what she was about to say next.

"As you know, I am a psychic and an energy healer."

"Psychic! What is that, then? Is it a disease or something?" said James, who was taking the mickey.

"Now, now, cheeky chops." Aunt Agatha put her arm around the inquisitive youngster.

"No, James," laughed Aunt Agatha. "A psychic is someone who is very sensitive or intuitive, which means the same, to everything around them - sounds, touch, smells, emotions, anger and love, and when anyone is depressed, I can sense it and feel compassion for them. I can also see auras around people which tells me a lot about them. Anyway, enough about that as it would take me forever explaining it all." She stopped for breath, watching the looks of interest on their faces.

"The plans I have are for turning Angel's Den into my healing sanctuary, so that I can heal people who need it, and also give guidance to those people who, of course, are willing to come and see me. I would have to advertise in the local paper until I become known in the area, or established, as they say. Now, there is more. Are you still interested?"

"Yes, of course." They all spoke softly as Aunt Agatha got comfy in her leather armchair.

"I would see the children off to school and be here for Katy as she is no trouble to me, are you, pet? And you will soon be starting infant school; only five months to go. Eee, you will soon grow up." Aunt Agatha patted Katy's head as the little girl looked up to the special person she worshipped. "Could I watch you doing your sidekick work?" asked Katy. Her aunt's face was a picture, and they all burst out laughing.

"Of course, you can, as I know you will be good and will pick up what I do very quickly, so you can be my apprentice."

Katy was bursting with pride and felt so important as she always did in Aunt Agatha's company.

"Any objections to my plans, then?"

"No!" they all shouted in unison.

"Cheers, big ears." James ducked to miss his dad's clout. "Enough of your cheek, boy." Secretly, David loved his son's sense of humour.

"No way, hozay." He was getting carried away now.

His dad looked over and raised his eyebrows which told James, enough is enough.

Aunt Agatha's bedroom was next to Angel's Den, so she was delighted at her workshop being nearby. She could stay up till late and just drop into her bed when she felt like it. Yes, just the job. Agatha rubbed her hands together; she was very content with her new life.

Everything was running smoothly at Maple Manor as Aunt Agatha had employed jolly fifty-year-old Mrs Banks as the cook, and a young cleaner called Sarah who attended college three afternoons a week studying art, who was almost desperate for the extra cash. She was a lovely eighteen-year-old and very easy to get on with.

Then there was Lenny, the old gardener, who also knew a lot about horses as well as plants, so this was a bonus for Dione. Things were going to plan.

Aunt Agatha and her little family were happy at Maple Manor.

Excitement was growing in the Bex household as there was a surprise in store for two lucky people.

"The men are here with the horses. Please, Sarah, please open the door so I can see them properly."

Katy could not get out of the door quick enough; she nearly tripped herself up.

"Watch out, clumsy clogs," chuckled Sarah who adored little Katy as they got on very well.

The horses were for Dione and James as a present as they shared the same birthday, and as Katy was now at infant school and finished earlier, Mum had allowed her to be in on the big treat in store for her brother and sister.

Dione was now fourteen years old, and James was twelve. Nat shook her head sadly. *Aunt is right - they soon grow up. It does not seem five minutes since we moved here.* Nat felt uneasy and shivered as if something was going to go wrong.

Oh, it's me being a silly old fool, she thought and hurried outside to be there for the children when they arrived home. The last three years had flown by.

As Dione and James came up the path, they were overjoyed at seeing the horses.

"Wicked! Wicked! Thanks, Mum, thanks, Aunty." they both threw their arms around their horses. *Typical,* thought Aunt Agatha, *that's kids for you.*

"White one is mine, so there." Dione made sure she got that in before James.

"I don't care, mine looks like Black Beauty who used to be on the telly. Anyway, mine's a boy and will be called Blackie."

"Sounds as if you had a baby," howled Katy as she danced around both of them." "Happy birthday, Dione and James, hip, hip, hooray. Happy birthday to you," their younger sister sang in a delightful voice and they applauded her.

Katy had become a lovely child since Agatha had come into her life and was an excellent pupil at school, good at everything she did, and most popular with her friends. Of course, there was always one bully in the class but that did not bother her, as she could handle Sadie Frost. Besides, with her intuitive powers, Katy knew that deep down the bully was insecure and needed to feel important. *Shame really* thought Katy. *If only Sadie would stop being on the defensive and allow her nice side to shine through, she would be as popular as I am.* The blonde-haired youngster felt so confident that she wanted to share it.

She felt quite proud of herself and went indoors to help prepare the party food. She liked to help Mrs Banks, the cook, who appreciated it, and in turn, was teaching this now delightful child how to cook.

Katy was also interested in herbs and flowers, along with plants that had healing properties too. Nearly six years old, this young lady was fascinated with the work that her Aunt Agatha did and was always in a hurry to join her when she was dealing with clients who were unwell or depressed and needed someone to lift their spirits up. Aunt Agatha treated them by giving them some hands-on healing using the energies that are all around in the atmosphere; hard to believe but so true.

Her aunt used lots of different herbal remedies but always insisted that her clients saw their own doctor if an imbalance remained that she could not heal, which did not happen very often.

There was so much to learn, and Katy absorbed it all and had a great thirst for learning more. There were not enough hours in the day for school and all this alternative healing and psychic work. It really surprised her where the time went.

Aunt Agatha's computer was delivered very quickly, as she had only ordered it online on James's mobile phone three days ago and she felt it all a bit daunting. It was like a new world for her.

"Pet, come here a minute and help me with this dumb machine, as I can't suss it out. And another thing, how am I going to write to my friends with this new email? I will not know their new addresses, and anyway, where do I stick the postage stamps?" It will take me forever with all this technology; you can keep it."

By this time, Katy was in stitches laughing at her elderly aunt.

"You are so funny, Aunt Agatha. Sorry for laughing but it's not as difficult as you think; you will soon pick it up, and I will help you. All you need to know is how to keep files on your clients, your password and, first of all, how to turn your computer off and on, how to open an email, how to save it or delete it, and how to reply to your clients if need be. Your email addresses will be saved, so no need to worry about losing any contacts."

"Yes, pet, I want to know how to get on the net as long as I don't have to do any fishing or stupid surfing as I can't even swim."

Katy tried to stifle a giggle at her aunt's funny statements and they both ended up in fits of laughter on the floor.

"How about eventually setting up a web page?" suggested Katy to her bemused aunt, who felt she was out of her depth as it was all new to her.

"A web page? What?! And have spiders running all over the place? I don't think so."

"Aunt Agatha, stop it. My jaws are aching." She held her face in her hands, her eyes sparkled with laughter and young Katy had tears streaming down her cheeks. "Ha, ha, ha," she chuckled.

"Eee, it's good to see you so happy, pet. Come and give us a big love, then."

It was a wonderful feeling being wrapped up in those beefy arms of her affectionate aunt. The infant felt so secure and sighed with contentment.

"Now, Katy, let's get serious for a mo." Aunt Agatha sat with a straight face, trying to look serious.

"What will I call my website, pet?"

The excited five-year-old concentrated hard as she searched her mind for ideas.

"If it is for your psychic readings, you could name it - wait for it - crystal clear at psychic.com, or if it is for your healing work, how about Harmony healing at hands on.com?"

"Well done, Katy, I couldn't have done better myself. So, I will bear that in mind. Now, off you go and get yourself to bed as it's long past your bedtime."

This young girl has a very creative imagination, thought Aunt Agatha, who was proud of her niece. Then, she yawned, saying, "Time for my bed. I will ask her to set up my email tomorrow."

"Night, night, sleep tight, watch the bugs don't bite." Agatha stifled her mouth with her hand as she was still yawning.

"See you in the morning, pet."

"Night, night, Aunt Agatha, love you." Making her way to bed, she rubbed her sleepy eyes, thinking of how much she was looking forward to school in the morning. She certainly did have a thirst for learning, which is a sign of intelligence.

Chapter 6.
School and Healing Arts

"Sadie Frost! Did you hear me or am I talking to a brick wall?" Miss Davey, the art teacher, was fuming at the trick Sadie Frost had played on Claire Hill, who was one of the shyest girls in the school.

She had scribbled all over Claire's beautiful painting which she had finished for her art exam, hoping to get top marks as the artwork was spectacular.

"What gets into your mind to make you do these horrible things, girl?" "I don't know," muttered Sadie. She avoided the teacher's eyes and looked as if she could not give a damn.

"Detention again, Sadie! How many more times this week, girl?"

Young Katy mimicked the teacher; "How many more times, girl?"

"Mind your own beeswax, Katy Bex, or I'll smack you in the gob, okay?" Sadie thought she was tough and acted it out to make all the school think she was hard, but she was a coward.

"Sadie Frost! Out now to the headmaster's room for detention."

Sadie scowled at Katy with venom in her voice and threatened, "You wait till after school."

"For what?" Katy answered bravely, as she put her paintbrushes back into her school desk, whistling happily to herself. This child had no fear or anger in her. She had been in school now for nearly five years and knew this bully inside and out.

Sadie Frost had a cruel streak in her nature and could not wait to get her own back on this girl.

Hiding round the corner of the local toffee shop, she knew Katy would be coming out at lunchtime for sweets, and waited, impatiently, ready to pounce.

"Right, teacher's pet! Let's see how clever you are without all your friends." Crack! She smacked Katy across her face with her fist, and Katy felt herself go down onto the pavement like a tonne of bricks.

"Ouch! That hurt!" she murmured to herself, as she did not want the bully to think that she was frightened of her.

Picking herself up, she shouted, "Sticks and stones will break my bones, but you will never hurt me." *That did not sound right,* thought Sadie, but she got the impression that Katy Bex was not frightened of her, and she was fighting a losing battle.

"So, you think because you live in that big posh house that you are better than me, you little snob!"

"I have never been a snob," Katy replied and realised it was Sadie who felt inferior to her. She felt sorry for her.

"My mum always said that manners and treating others as you like to be treated go a long way in life and remember, you do not frighten me, Miss Frost, with your bully-boy tactics. Nice people are much more important to me than those with lots of money so why do you want to try and harm me, Miss Frost?"

Katy was being sarcastic.

Sadie was fuming as she slowly backed away from Katy. *Oh well, there is always Claire to pick on; that will make me feel good,* she tried to convince herself as she spied the shy eight-year-old girl who was trying to hide from her.

Claire was petrified and was trying to run away from her, but it was no use; she took a large breath in.

Sadie had her pinned against the playground wall. No one noticed, as the rest of the class were busy watching stocky Danny Jones, who was another eight-year-old, bullying timid six-year-old Adam Black who had a bad squint in his eye that he was so self-conscious of, and he tried to cover his eyes with one of his hands.

Meanwhile, nine-year-old Frosty Face, as Sadie was called behind her back, was really laying the law down as she swept her frizzy hair back out of her green eyes, tucking it behind her ears.

"Listen to me, stupid Eclaire. Do as you are told and I won't pick on you again, cross my heart and hope to die." Ginger-haired Sadie was good at lying. It was second nature to her. "God forgive you, Sadie Frost," said Claire, who shivered with fear as she was being forced to do something that was very wrong. Her brown eyes were wide with fear.

"I am not stealing Katy's mobile phone. No, I w-w-won't do it," she stammered." She is the best friend in the world to me." The slim, fair-haired girl wanted to be left alone.

"Make me," she said defiantly. Tears ran down her cheeks, and she was shivering uncontrollably, trying to be strong.

"Ha! Best friend? What a load of rubbish! Get that phone for me or you will be very, very sorry, Eclaire."

Sadie punched the shy girl on the arm and strutted away shouting, "You have got until tomorrow, girl, or else," she threatened.

Claire tucked her fine fair hair back into her hat, which Sadie had knocked off her head, and made her way back to the classroom, shaking as she walked past Danny Jones as he threw his weight about with intimidating words and cruel actions.

"Speak up, specky four-eyes! Come on, speak up, smelly Adam! Has the cat got your tongue or something?" The smaller boy backed off, but Danny was quick off the mark.

Danny was a cocky lad and expected everyone to cheer him, but just as he pulled Adam's spectacles off his face, Katy came round the corner and shouted out, "At least

Adam's eyes will get better through wearing his spectacles, but you will always be a horrible person! Go on, pick on someone your own size."

The crowds who surrounded Danny started chanting, "Bully-boy Jones, bully-boy Jones."

"Come on, don't get upset. He isn't worth it, Adam," said Katy. "He has to show off to feel important; shame really. Ah, bless." Katy helped Adam to calm down.

Danny went red and felt stupid in front of his mates. "I will get you back, just wait, Katy Bex," he mumbled.

Home at last, Katy skipped into the garden to see what the gardener was up to.

Lenny, the gardener, looked ever so worried as he ran to the big house. "Agatha, Agatha! Come quickly and help! Give us a hand with Blackie as he is not eating again."

Lenny was flustered as he thought the horse could be dying.

"That's been four days now. I know that the vet will only tell me to give him a few more days but I am concerned as he looks ever so poorly."

Agatha was followed quickly by her nine-year-old niece who did not like to miss out on the action. Blackie was ever so miserable, and he had a dark cloud around him as her heart went out to this lovely sick animal who was lying on the stable floor.

"Aunt, what is that dark cloud around Blackie?" "That, my dear, is not a cloud but is called an aura, and it is dark and very murky."

Katy noticed that Blackie did not look well at all and felt so sorry for him. She wanted to help him get better.

"What does it mean?" Katy was desperate to know as she felt that the horse was failing fast.

"My dear girl, the aura is an electrical force field of energy which surrounds all living things, be they animal, plant, mineral or human. When the energy is low, that is when the aura becomes dull like. That tells me that his life force is leaving the body, so, we must bring the energy in that will help him."

"And how do we do that, Aunt Agatha?" Katy was puzzled.

"Run your hands above Blackie's back and you should feel a tingling sensation. If it is not smooth, that is when you have to bring in the energies from the universe, down through your hands, so, Katy, ask your Angels for help to give Blackie good healing energies to make him well again."

Agatha watched; she knew that Katy was a natural receiver of energy to heal this poor horse and that this would be the first time for Katy. This was all going over Lenny's head as he thought it was a right load of mumbo jumbo. "I can't see any black, Miss Agatha."

"You're not a sensitive, that's why, Lenny. Nothing wrong with you, like, just some people have it and some don't."

"Now, madam, how are you doing, pet?"

"Oh, what a wonderful feeling of warmth in my hands! It feels like magic; is it, Aunt, is it magic? And I can see purple. It must be magic."

"No, lass, it is an old art that we have nearly lost over the years and the purple you can see is a healing energy, but that is another story. Anyway, how is Blackie, poor boy?"

Aunt Agatha stroked the horse's mane and was delighted that his immediate response to the young girl's gentle touch, was to try to reach her hands as he lifted his head slowly off the straw-covered floor.

He stretched forward towards his bag of oats. "Good boy, good boy, and well done, Katy."

Agatha was over the moon. She knew Katy had it in her - she had lots of healing and intuitive gifts, but she was also very clever at school and loved learning. Auntie knew that her education was more important at this time in her life, but who knows what the future holds?

Agatha was quite excited at the thought.

After all the drama that Katy had been part of, it was time to change out of her school uniform or she would get earache off her Mum, however, Nat had bought a surprise present for her daughter, as she had been so well behaved, and she wanted to encourage her to stay that way.

"Wow, Mum, it's absolutely wicked! Look what I've got, Jamie." Katy was dancing around, waving the surprise in front of her older brother. "Don't you think it's sweet, Jamie?"

"Don't call me Jamie, ok? It's James to you, little sister, alright?"

He was growing up fast and his voice had deepened.

Misery guts! It's only a name." Katy danced around her brother waving the mobile phone which had been promised to her for her ninth birthday, but she had received it earlier. "It's better than yours; I can download all sorts of things onto this one." She was annoying him now, but James decided to ignore her.

Monster Mash stuck out her tongue, her eyes sparkling in devilment but in a nice way.

"Leave her alone, James. She is a lot younger than you and you are, after all, a teenager now." Mum was getting fed up with both of them now.

James didn't feel like a teenager as he was only four foot six inches in height and had been for a long time. "Why are my mates bigger than me, Mum? It's not fair." "Listen, son, good things come in small parcels. Stop worrying as you don't stop growing till you are twenty-one."

"God, that's forever," sighed James.

"It will go quicker than you think, my young man," Mum assured him, stroking his thick dark hair, and she lovingly gave her son a big cuddle, which, of course, he enjoyed deep down. He knew he was still Mummy's boy.

James and Dione both had cool mobiles, so he wasn't bothered at all. They had iPhones, but Katy did not know the difference at her age.

"Anything to keep baby face happy," he said sarcastically, as he gave Katy a sly look. If the truth be known, he was still jealous of his sister but tried to hide it, as he did not want the rest of the family taking the mickey.

"I cannot wait to show my new mobile off at school."

Katy was so pleased with it that she clapped her hands and kissed her Mum who thought, *That is a first.*

Chapter 7.
The Great Loss

"Katy Bex, you are not paying attention! That's not like you. Come on, girl, you can normally reach the top notes of the scale. Whatever is the matter?"

Miss Brown, the music teacher, put her hand out to the confused child and Katy started to cry. "Miss, I don't know. I keep getting a horrible feeling in my tummy, but I don't feel sick, just ice cold." She felt that there was something wrong somewhere.

Miss could not understand it as Katy was not up to her usual high standards in the music lesson, and her dancing had been a disaster too.

Must just be an off day for her, mused the teacher.

"Never mind, dear, you have probably picked up a virus and might feel better in the morning, I'm sure. Anyway, it's home time, so off you go."

Katy made her way to the cloakroom to get her jacket and slowly made her way out of school. She just wanted to feel secure at home with her family.

"Now, what have I done with Mr Battie's file?" whispered Agatha, as if someone could hear her.

She was working in Angel's Den, as usual, every hour that God sent.

He has arthritis in his knees. I am not surprised with his job as a carpet fitter he could do with looking for a new job, she thought.

Eucalyptus oil - that should do the trick.

Her chubby body reached up to a high shelf for aromatherapy oil, then suddenly, Agatha felt a sharp pain tightening across her chest.

"Suffering ice cakes!" The elderly lady groaned and rolled forward onto the thick pile carpet.

"Please, please, someone help me, please," Aunt Agatha gasped.

Everything went black as Agatha struggled to breathe. The elderly lady eventually tried to get herself up from the floor and found it so difficult that she just lay there praying.

Meanwhile, Nat had not been able to settle in work and decided to come home early, as she also had a migraine, which was becoming worse as the morning wore on.

"I knew there was something wrong!" Nat exclaimed and she wrung her hands as she found her dear aunt lying unconscious on the floor in Angel's Den, her face a bluish-grey and looking so vulnerable. Nat placed a fleecy blanket over Agatha.

Within minutes, blue flashing lights and sirens came whistling. It was a nightmare for Nat as she hoped Aunt Agatha would pull through this. She held her hand, gently reassuring her that she would be fine.

"Won't be long now, Agatha. We will soon be at the hospital. Hang on in there." Nat tried to calm her aunt who looked terrible, her skin now the colour of a waxen candle.

There was no sign of any response from her aunt as they wheeled her into intensive care.

Nat had to leave as Agatha was settled into bed, tubes everywhere. "Picking Katy up from school. I won't be long; luv you," she said as she hurried out.

"I tried to phone you, Katy, but could not get through." She didn't want to shock her daughter by putting her arms around her as Katy was not used to close comfort from Mum.

Nat realised that Katy had not heard a word and the pale young girl knew it was bad news but was unaware that her brand new mobile phone was missing.

The least of her worries.

Sadness crept into Nat's voice. "Please save her, please hear my prayers." But she knew deep down that the aunt would not survive.

The family sat huddled together in the small pink-walled ward, all eyes on their aunt, who had been in a coma now for two days. The doctors did not hold out much hope for her, as she had had a massive heart attack, which had done irreparable damage.

The family knew it was only a matter of time.

"Time you all went home for some rest," demanded the night sister.

"There isn't anything anyone can do, as it is in God's hands now."

Katy would not let go of her aunt and clung to her like super glue.

The night nurse felt ever so sorry for this little girl. She had been in shock for the last two days and this was the first sound she had made; *She obviously means a lot to the child,* the nurse thought.

"Come on, we will make up a bed for you at the side of your precious aunt."

"Yes, yes, thank you, nurse!" Katy was so happy that she hugged the nurse as she waved the family off. "Bye, take care," she shouted.

Katy settled down and watched Aunt Agatha until she was so tired herself that she fell asleep. However, she was awake again at three and it was so dark that weary Katy turned on a small light to comfort her.

Wondering what that noise was, Katy strained her ears to hear what was going on and sat up suddenly as she knew her aunt was struggling with her breathing now, even though she had an oxygen mask on. She was also trying to speak;

"K-k-kaaaty, will w-w-will you..." Her aunt's voice was very weak as she placed her hands on the emerald necklace which she never removed, even if she was having a bath. It was an ancient necklace that had been given to her when she was an aid worker in Africa by a young wise man called Machu.

That was all Katy and the family had knowledge of and they had never, ever questioned it.

Flippin' 'eck! Aunt wants me to take it off her neck; she must want me to have it, thought Katy.

Katy carefully removed the jewellery from her aunt's tired body, finding it difficult, with all the wires and tubes. She felt her aunt give a big sigh.

She sounds relieved, Katy thought, not realising that Aunt Agatha was about to take her last breath.

"I will look after this for you, Aunt Agatha, as I know how much you treasure it."

Reassuring her aunt, Katy placed the necklace around her own neck, tucking it into her lilac jacket to keep it safe.

There was a beautiful smile on Aunt Agatha's face, like a ray of sunshine, but it suddenly changed to a look of complete bewilderment, and Agatha became very irritated.

After she made her aunt's bed a bit more comfortable by straightening the duvet, young Katy slipped quietly into her small bed at the side of Agatha's, unaware that her beloved aunt had passed away. "Look, nurse, can you see the lovely colours floating around Auntie's head? They look like tiny dancing stars, no, stardust, that's what it is, magical, isn't it?" Katy was mesmerised.

"Stardust, mmm," the nurse muttered, wondering what the child could have seen around her aunt. Strange girl.

"Can you see it?" Katy said excitedly as she leaned over towards her aunt.

The nurse felt the patient's pulse then gently moved Katy out of the tiny ward into a side office.

Moving into another room, the nurse contacted the family to break the tragic news.

Katy wore a perplexed look as she could hear snippets of the conversation with her parents. It was a sorrowful time for them all.

The wind howled through the churchyard, in through the small, tightly packed church and into the heart of the golden haired little girl. Eight-year-old Katy sobbed uncontrollably as the grief enfolded her and she cried out, "Aunt Agatha, why have you deserted me? I feel so lonely without your special love."

Her aunt's casket was placed gently onto the platform which was overflowing with flowers. Many people had come to pay their respects. There were friends, neighbours and relatives, all of whom had loved her very much. It was a sad day. No one realised just how much it would affect young Katy.

There were floral tributes, of all colours and shapes, placed around the wooden casket. One display in particular stood out from the others. It was a round green ball of herbs. This was Katy's gift given with lots of love and was symbolic of Aunt Agatha's working life as a fortune teller and healer who, over many years, had helped many a sick person with her herbal remedies and her counselling.

Katy felt as if a sheet of ice had wrapped itself around her heart. *Why have you left me?* she cried inwardly. Things would never be the same for this child, and her life was going to change dramatically and lessons were to be learned.

Katy's parents looked at each other in disbelief as they tried to console their distraught daughter.

They hoped that she would come through this.

David was at his wit's end with her as it was the third time in four days that he'd had to ground Katy for being naughty.

"Don't you realise what you are putting us all through? Hey, when are you going to behave yourself?"

"Whatever." Katy shrugged her shoulders with a couldn't-care-less attitude and dumped her school bag onto the floor of her untidy bedroom, kicked her shoes off and put her hands over her ears to block out her father's voice.

"He is a muppet and he is getting on my nerves. Who does he think he is, a sergeant major? Yes, Sir." She saluted him with anger and sarcasm in her voice.

"Do as Daddy say or else?" She laughed into David's face.

Katy had become the child from hell again, but this time, David and Nat were dealing with a grieving nine-year-old, not a baby. He was at his wit's end with her.

"It's like the mobile phone that you lost; do you think money grows on trees?" Dad was losing his temper now and had to control himself, as he felt like really shaking some sense into his daughter. That was out of character for him, it would be wrong, and it would not solve anything.

"Grounded for a month, ok, Katy? Again."

Katy stuck her tongue out behind her dad's back knowing that he would have gone mad had he seen her do it. She knew it was disrespectful but was not bothered about him.

"I am so unhappy," she moaned as the sobbing Katy climbed into bed and huddled under the pink duvet, hiding herself from the world. She could feel her heart breaking in two with sadness.

"I hope I see Aunt Agatha again. I miss her so much."

Katy cried herself to sleep that night.

The young girl's heart turned into an iceberg that nothing would melt.

In the last twelve months, she had painted her dad's car with red paint. She had let James and Dione's horses out of their paddock and Blackie had to be put down after a car struck him. James was devastated at the loss.

She had exchanged the glue Nat used to mend things at home for a super glue that had bonded Nat's fingers together, and after struggling to prise them open, she had taken skin off the top of her fingers and had to go to the local hospital for medical help.

Katy was unruly at school, fell behind in all of her lessons and her attitude was abhorrent.

Mum and Dad were at the end of their tether.

Chapter 8.
Crystal Ball and Planet of Light

Katy welcomed the night as it was a comfort to her, for when darkness came, all the rest of the family were in bed, hopefully asleep, and Katy could visit her new retreat.

The nine-year-old quietly slipped into Angel's Den, as she treated this as a shrine to her aunt, and a sanctuary for herself. She had begun to hate her family with a vengeance.

Grief-stricken, Katy had been coming in here every night since her beloved aunt had died over nine months ago, and she felt nearer to her, and her work. This was a haven for the young girl, bringing her peace. "Let's see if there are any emails, as there must be some people who don't know yet about Aunt Agatha passing away." Katy shook her head sadly.

She wanted to contact all her customers so that they could pay their last respects to her much-loved aunt. She owed her that at least.

"I could answer them, yes, I will be helping Aunt Agatha in some way."

Click, click, she pressed the keys searching for any emails.

"Hang on, there's a message; let me have a closer look."

Katy was becoming quite excited as the screen lit up and she began to read the emails. *Better stop talking, as I might wake up the family,* Katy thought.

To Agatha @ crystal clear.com.uk ". Help us; we need your help; our world is incredibly sad as most of the light has gone, and our planet will die without your help. Please help, activate the crystal urgently."

From Magi, Keeper of Dreams @the Oracle.cloud.air Planet of Light.

This all sounds a bit strange, thought Katy. *I have never heard Aunt Agatha mention a Magi. But there again, she must have had a lot of contacts that I am not aware of.*

Katy quickly emailed Magi. Whoever or whatever it was, she was puzzled but knew by the plea that they were desperate for help.

'Don't know what to do, please help me to understand your message,' she typed the words, worrying as she did so.

'How can I activate the crystal?' from crystal clear.com.uk over and out.

Eventually, a message came through.

'Log on to Keeper of Dreams for instructions, Okay dokey, cheers,' from Magi.

"Keeper of Dreams." Katy placed the cursor into the box. "Here goes." She pressed and clicked the mouse. Nothing; no response whatsoever.

Katy tried all the different buttons and nothing happened. She was becoming so frustrated, as she had sat up most of the night.

She waited eagerly but got no reply whatsoever.

Night after night, she spent in Angel's Den with no contact reaching her and eventually, she decided to give up again and went to bed so very disappointed.

About three nights later, Katy was going to the bathroom and was aware of a droning noise coming from Angel's Den. She could not ignore it as it was so loud.

She felt an inner fear of something that did not feel right but sensed a compulsion to be drawn into the fear of the unknown, so to speak. "Please, Aunt Agatha, stay by my side," she pleaded, with a sudden awareness that something was about to change her future.

As she walked towards her aunt's room, she saw a green light pulsating from under the door, and as she opened the door, she was astounded at what she saw.

Her aunt's crystal ball, which was at the side of the computer, was throwing out an eerie glow and looked as if it had come to life. It was making a humming noise that rattled in Katy's brain making her dizzy.

The orb was sending out waves of luminous green light, and Katy moved closer, peering into this large crystal ball that was placed at the side of Aunt Agatha's computer.

Katy was apprehensive as she approached it, and felt the hairs stand up on the back of her neck.

Even though she was frightened, she knew that she had to go through with this, and in her mind, she asked for help from Aunt Agatha.

As Katy stared into the ball, there in the mistiness stood a person in brown robes beckoning Katy towards him, and his voice was pleading, "Come closer, come closer." She leaned forward to hear him clearer as his voice became a whisper.

Suddenly, Woosh! Katy was being sucked into the crystal and was propelled into the depths of it with an alarming speed, deep into the unknown that lay beyond. "Help!" she cried, but no one could hear her, as the Bex household were all asleep.

The terrified young girl felt like she was going through a bright white tunnel. The colours which swirled around Katy were so dazzling, that she protected her eyes with both hands, as her mind was totally confused as to where she was going. It seemed to last forever, and the frightened youngster wished it would be over soon, as she was panicking now.

Someone must have read her mind as, in a flash, there was a change of pace and the atmosphere changed immediately.

Bump! "Ow, ow, that hurts," Katy screamed as her bottom hit the mound of rough wet soil. "Where am I?"

She opened her eyes and squinted through the greyness around her.

She could vaguely see a figure standing in front of her, but the outline was mistier than her surroundings.

Strange, thought Katy, who was apprehensive now, and wrapped her arms around herself, feeling insecure.

"Well, well, who have we got here then?" The brown-robed figure stepped forward, bending down to help Katy.

The nine-year-old seemed lost and didn't seem to know where she was, but eventually, the robed figure took her hand in his.

"Get off me, ya muppet!" snarled Katy and dragged her hand away from the old monk whose gentle brown eyes were puzzled at Katy's behaviour.

"Who are you anyway, and what are you doing here?

And another thing," Katy was becoming hysterical, "where am I?"

"Calm down, dear." The older gent put his arm around Katy, helping her to stand up.

"You, my girl, are here on an important mission and people's dreams are depending on you."

"I don't understand." Katy was really frightened now and started to shiver violently.

"Just relax and breathe slowly, please, slowly, that's the way."

The monk held the now-calm Katy's hand.

"I am Dominic, the Keeper of Dreams, and I have been waiting for you to contact us here, on the Planet of Light. You have interfered with our karma and caused chaos, so, sorry, we had to bring you here."

"What do you mean? Why? What have I done?" Katy was worried now and tried to concentrate on what the old monk was saying, thinking it is a load of rubbish.

"Young lady, you had no right to remove your aunt's necklace, the Emerald Key, as it was her destiny to bring it to us on her passing to the spirit world nearly a year ago now."

"No, no, don't blame me for it, as my wonderful aunt made me aware that she wanted me to have it. So there, stick that in your pipe and smoke it." Katy was wound up by now and thought this was all a nightmare that she would wake up from.

"Listen, my dear Katy, just sit still and listen to a story I have to tell you, then you may understand why you have been brought here."

"Whatever." Katy scowled as she squinted her eyes at the monk. "This better be good, and I am listening."

"Many years ago, when your Aunt Agatha was a missionary worker in Africa, she befriended a wise man call Machu, who taught her many things." Dominic hoped that this young lady would understand and accept what had happened.

"That bit I know." Katy screwed her face and wondered what was coming next.

"The wise man had been given the Emerald Key when he was a boy of ten, by an older sage who made this amulet, and with his spells of love, gave it special magical qualities of power that mend all forms of broken and sick souls back to being whole again and brings in the love and light."

"Why was h-h-he…" Katy stammered.

"Please listen until I finish. The ancient necklace has healing properties and is always passed onto those who are incredibly special on Earth, who do good works. However, we did not expect the Planet of Light ever to be hit with such an unknown disaster, and that is why we had to bring Agatha from Earth, and free her physical body, for her to come over to our world with the necklace.

Our planet is on the brink of dying without the healing energies, and that is why it is so dark here.

We are so terribly worried that we are now running out of time. There are many sick souls here who need healing before they can rise above to a higher plane called Nirvana. "The wise monk hoped Katy would understand.

"Why didn't the wise man take it over when he died? If what you say is true, tell me that, then!" she retorted.

Katy was no dummy and waited for an answer.

"Well, dear, the wise man was in a bad accident. He was crushed by elephants and your aunt gave everything she had to save this dear friend who was only thirty years old at the time.

My dad is only forty, Katy thought and could not imagine her life without him, ever. Dominic could see that he held the child's interest and continued with the story.

"Your aunt nursed him for three months, but unfortunately, his wounds were so bad that even Machu knew he did not have long for this world.

He always sensed that your aunt had a caring nature, and he told her the story of the Emerald Key and asked if he could entrust it to her keep, as he did not think that the Planet of Light would ever need it. However, Agatha could take the Emerald Key and its magical powers when she did make her final journey from the Earth plane, even though the Planet of Light was thriving, and at least the key would be with the Keeper of Dreams just in case there was ever a catastrophe. Unfortunately, that is what happened not long after your aunt passed away without the Emerald Key on her person that would have prevented the Planet of Light from being in this shocking situation.

Therefore, my dear, you should have left it with your aunt, as we would have had the Emerald Key here when the disaster struck. That is why we were so desperate to contact you. However, it is not your fault; you did not know, little one." He noticed her sadness and patted her on the head, which Katy hated, but she reacted by asking, "So, what will happen now?"

"Because your aunt did not have the key on her when she came to this plane, we are rapidly losing daylight, however, we have the key now to open the Crystal Caves, which will unlock the healing energies, restoring the planet's light and when that's done, you can go back home.

"You are our guardian angel, Katy, and don't forget that, my dear."

Dominic waited for a response from this angry-looking child standing there in her pink pyjamas.

"Hmm, well, that's that, then." Katy folded her arms in front of herself to feel warmer.

As Katy lifted the Emerald Key from around her neck to pass it to Dominic, there was suddenly a flutter of wings.

Out of the greyness appeared a jackdaw who swooped down among the three figures surprising them all.

"Caw, caw, I'll have that, thank you very much." said the bird, grabbing the necklace out of Katy's reach, and flying away at lightning speed, its wings flapping nineteen to the dozen.

"Oh, my goodness." Dominic went pale and felt his legs go weak as he struggled to keep his balance. He collapsed into a heap and put his head in his hands, rocking back and forward with fear.

Katy was so distracted by her thoughts, that she was unaware of being watched from afar.

Chapter 9.
Friends and Foe

"Magi, wipe the oracle now." The dark orb was covered in dust and cobwebs, as it had not been used for such a long time.

Aunt Agatha was sick with worry when she had arrived at Magi's den, and screeched at him again, "Clean it."

She could not believe the danger young Katy was getting into and rubbing her hands nervously, she immediately checked out the oracle, which was like a shining black sphere.

"Is that better?" Magi had used his cape-like sleeves to clear the mistiness from the crystal.

"Yes," smiled Aunt Agatha. "I can keep my eyes on my beloved Katy to make sure she is safe from harm."

Aunt Agatha felt a bit peckish and turned to the magician. "Magi, put the kettle on and make some blueberry tea, and I will have your homemade Juniper Berry cakes with all the scrumptious juice oozing out. Yum."

Agatha licked her lips in anticipation.

In between stuffing themselves with food and drink, the jolly aunt had a sudden thought! *I am becoming selfish in my old age,* mused Agatha as she licked her sticky fingers and slurped her blueberry tea down hastily.

"Now, let us see how Katy is getting on."

They both peered intently into the oracle, ready for any rescue work if needed.

Agatha was so grateful to her email friend, Magi the Magician, for when she was making her journey to the Planet of Light, he had intercepted her to protect her from the evil Huccanites, and directed her to his cave, away from danger, which she had not been aware of. She was safe here until it was time to leave for the Halls of Healing which heal all souls of illnesses and pain, so they can enjoy the Planet of Light forever, finding Nirvana, which is enlightenment of all knowledge, and becoming a pure soul for eternity.

Meanwhile, as Katy stood in disbelief of all that was happening, out of a clearing in the hedge emerged a colourful image of a clown-like being who hastily introduced himself.

"Hi, I'm Art and as you can see, I love colours, hence the cloak." He laughed as he swirled the rainbow coat of different hues around himself.

"I could not help overhearing your conversation, so I apologise, but I can offer you some help if you wish; is it a deal, then?" He peered closely at the two figures in front of him, not knowing what their answer would be.

Dominic eyed the happy soul up and down, pleased with the trust in this boy's face. "A deal it is, young man! Welcome aboard and thank you." The monk shook Art's hand warmly which made the youth feel that at least the old monk had taken to him and accepted him as a friend.

"Who is this forlorn bundle of rags, then?" Art squinted at Katy's small, pathetic appearance, feeling quite sorry for her as her nightclothes were covered in mud where she had fallen on her arrival to the Planet of Light.

"Mind your own beeswax!" shouted Katy as she tried to straighten her creased dirty pyjamas and blushed furiously.

"Now, now, children, let's not go there, as we have more things to worry about that are important." Dominic wanted to keep the peace; he needed to calm Katy down, as he could feel the young girl's hostility towards Art. *She is very touchy and should be handled carefully,* thought the wise monk.

"Art, spit it out - what can you tell us?" Dominic was becoming impatient as time was running out, and the sooner they got their plan off the ground the better.

"The jackdaw, Grabb is his name, will have flown to the Forest of Shadows, as that is where he hides all his stolen goods and it is so dark in there, no one would find his treasure."

Scratching his head, Art watched for a reaction from the duo.

Katy blinked rapidly as she was becoming annoyed with this idiot of a so-called helper. "Well, how the heck are we going to find him if it is that dark, you silly person?"

"I have already thought of that," Art replied with a great big smile on his face, which Katy wanted to smack, but managed to keep her hands to herself.

"Look who I've got here in my pocket! Meet Silky the spider; he will be a great help, won't you, Silky?"

The tiny furry creature crawled out of Art's bright yellow pants, and peered through silky eyelashes, weighing up the strangers who had come closer to have a better look at him.

He was an absolutely beautiful little thing, thought Katy, but she made no comment as she shuffled back as if to let this tiny mite have some breathing space as he appeared to be very shy.

"H-h-hullo, everybody. Pleased t-t-to m-meet you."

Silky felt so embarrassed and was not used to being scrutinised by so many eyes.

Art stuck out his chest feeling a bit more important with his pet at his side and made a suggestion to the nasty young girl.

"Katy has a wonderful singing voice, and my friend here can move as quick as the speed of light, so this should be a good combination for success, don't you think?" He paused for some response from Miss Frosty Face, as there was sure to be some, and Art didn't have to wait long as she turned on him and snapped, "What?! How did you find out about my singing?" Katy quizzed Art, as she wrapped her arms tightly round her tiny frame.

She was angry at being called Frosty Face as it reminded her of Sadie Frost, and Art did not know that she could read his mind.

His mind - oh my goodness! What is happening to me? Am I that bad? Why can I not behave and be who I once was, when Aunt Agatha was beside me? The poor girl was still angry.

"Well, clever clogs, where is your plan, then?" Katy was trying to provoke Art, but he was ready for her.

"There is a lot I know about you, mark my words," he grinned. "I keep my eye on every being as they learn on the Earth plane, and, young lady, I happen to know everything about you." He stroked Silky and sat down on a nearby rock.

"Yeah, whatever." Katy shrugged her shoulders and did not really believe him; well, there was a tiny bit of doubt.

I wonder if he saw me trying to drown Topsy, no I don't think so, Katy thought, then she waited for more from this intriguing youth.

"We only have one hour of sunshine to find our way to this Forest of Shadows and be safe from predators." He paused.

So, do we agree that Silky will spin his silken thread to guide us? Then this is where you come in, Katy."

The tired Katy was all ears now; *well, none of us are perfect, are we?* she giggled while settling herself on the mound of grass she had fallen on. *Stupid me, I forgot the mud.*

Standing upright, she tried to brush herself down, but it was a hopeless task as it was all over her.

She gave up in the end.

"Silky will wind his web along a pathway of shrubs, flowers and trees as he moves at a great speed, hopefully enabling us to find the Jackdaw quickly, and as you sing, Katy, the sound of the musical notes will vibrate the silken thread.

That way, as the sun disappears, the moon will shine its silver light onto the moving web as it glitters, directing us to the Forest of Shadows." Art looked smug.

"Well, I never." Dominic the Monk put his hands out to stroke the spider and moved his hands around till he found him.

Stroking him gently, he smiled. "Good idea."

Dominic was blind and no one knew, and the wise monk hoped it would stay that way as he could not cope with pity.

I wonder how things are at home? I bet no one misses me, Katy cried inwardly.

Little did she know that back on Earth, where none of Katy's friends knew of her disappearance yet, someone was planning their revenge on her.

She shivered and realised something was wrong but did not have a clue as she was too far away to tune into bully-boy Danny Jones and wicked Sadie Frost.

More to the point, she had other things to worry about; saving this planet, for a start.

That was her priority now, as she owed it to the sick people to make sure that she found the Key that would heal the planet, hopefully bringing in the light to heal all the broken souls. Katy felt it was her responsibility and she was determined to do all she could for them all.

Chapter 10.
Bullies Revenge

"Hah! I have got a surprise for Katy Bex and it won't be a nice one."

Danny Jones laughed as he was in his element after stealing Katy's mobile phone off Sadie Frost.

"I will delete all her numbers. Why should I care? Anyway, she's a right snobby cow. I'm sure she's from another planet; probably Planet of the Apes."

He chuckled as he tried to work out this new phone that he was not used to. "Hmm, pain in the bum," he snarled.

Little did he know she was on another planet, millions of miles away.

The bully roared with hysterics as he deleted one number after the other, enjoying his spiteful tactics.

Meanwhile, ginger-headed Sadie Frost was fuming after being robbed of the mobile phone. It was so cool; you could use it as a video camera and download all sorts of things from the internet such as music, YouTube, Facebook and many, many, apps and games.

She snarled, "I'll have to think of something else, something which will wind up stuck-up Katy even more.

Got it." she cried, and giggled mischievously to herself, pleased as punch. *Why am I so clever?!* She laughed as she thought of a so-called genius plot.

"There is that stupid book of so-called magic remedies that Katy has always got her nose buried in, something to do with that old biddy of an aunt who was teaching her all sorts of new-age rubbish. It gives me the heebie-jeebies." Sadie shivered as she sensed an ice-cold feeling rising up her spine.

"Yeah, I'll have to get my hands on it, the sooner the better. Hah! This will upset Miss Prim from the big Manor house. Love to see her face when she finds out." Sadie was in a great mood, whistling like a bird, her mind working overtime with the anticipation of planning just how to steal this special book that Miss Snobby had called her 'magic healing bible'.

"Claptrap," the stocky girl mumbled.

"Suppose I will have to go up to Maple Manor now we are on our school jolly's; hmm, I don't fancy that, so let me think." She scratched her head and frowned.

"Now, where is the chocolate Eclaire's phone number? Flicking through her own old mobile rapidly, Claire's number came up and Sadie made the call.

"Get here as soon as, or you will know the flippin'
consequences!" shouted Sadie. "I am counting - one, two,
three…"

Claire was there in five minutes, shaking as she walked
towards the girl who terrified her.

"Right, I hope you are ready for the break-in?"

"I c-can't do it." The blonde-haired, blue-eyed Claire
trembled with fear as Sadie dug her nails deep into Claire's
arm, demanding her to do as she was told.

Sadie was an expert at controlling others who were
basically, shy and she knew who to pick on. She was a
coward, as she never tackled anyone who could stand up to
her.

"What do you mean, you can't? I know you think you
can't, but believe me, you will." Digging her nails deeper
causing Claire's arm to bleed, she tugged at her hair,
shouting, "You be up at the big house tonight at nine
o'clock or else. I am warning you, Eclaire, let me down and
you will be sorry. You will live to regret it, mark my words,
if you live."

Sadie's eyes were full of evil as she yelled at the petrified girl
who was shaking from head to toe.

Frozen to the spot, Claire wiped away the tears which
tumbled down her pale cheeks.

" Ok, I will, I will do it." Her small figure shook with fear
and as she walked away, her legs nearly buckled under her
from the shock.

Sadie Frost had no idea that Katy was billions of miles away as she plotted her revenge against her.

No one knew she was missing.

"Have you seen Katy this morning?" asked Nat, who seemed anxious as she spoke to Mrs Banks the cook while trying to stop herself from overreacting.

"I haven't, luv. Last time I set eyes on her was at bedtime last night."

The old cook yawned.

"I hope she is not up to her old tricks, the little Madam." Mum was weary by now, wondering what Katy would do next.

"What, do you think so, Nat? Just to get attention like the old days? Never." The ruddy-faced Mrs Banks looked perplexed as she wiped her wet hands on her apron.

"Miss Katy surely grew out of that years ago, as you and David often talk about how naughty she was before her aunt turned up on your doorstep." Mrs Banks could see how distressed Nat was becoming, so the middle-aged lady placed her arms around the young mother's shoulders. "There now, I'm sure she will turn up."

"Katy became the child from hell again, Cook, when Aunt Agatha died, and only started to behave about a month ago." Panic was setting in as Nat struggled to breathe. Cook was getting on in years and did not have a clear memory of when Agatha had passed away.

Putting the dishes into the dishwasher, Cook turned to Nat; "Doesn't time fly? It does not seem like over seven years ago since I started working for lovely Agatha." Mentioning Aunt Agatha opened up old wounds of her never being with them again. Nat sobbed, "I don't know how Katy's brain ticks since Aunt Agatha has gone. I hope it is a silly game of hers, hiding just to get the attention. Anyway, let us see how long she can keep up with her silly antics, the stupid child."

Little did she know of the danger her precious daughter could be in.

"Shush! Creep up the stairs while the door is open. Hurry up, you clumsy lump."

Sadie pushed the timid girl towards the large oak front door, but Claire was paralysed with the shock of what she was expected to do and was frozen to the spot.

God, what's wrong with you, girl? Move it before I belt you round the earhole."

Claire would not budge and Sadie was beginning to panic.

"Someone might see me," the worried girl said, shaking like a leaf. She would not or could not go any further forward.

"Shove off, then." Burly Sadie pushed Claire aside and made her own way up the wide staircase, which was covered in a wonderful rich red carpet, not that Sadie noticed; there was too much on her mind.

She cunningly found her way to Katy's bedroom and searched quickly through her personal things on the bookcase while noticing the pink desk which was littered with papers. She frowned as she rubbed her forehead, mumbling, "Where the flipping heck does she keep this smelly book? It's not as if it's the crown jewels." Realising that she was talking out loud, the crafty ten-year-old kept her voice to herself but was becoming extremely irate when she heard a creak on the stairs. She knew that she would have to act speedily.

Looking around her, she spotted a bright pink bag sticking out of the open drawer of the desk, and quickly grabbed it. She then hid behind the door and held her breath as she clutched the bag to her chest.

It was only Sarah, the cleaning lady. She had stayed on with the Bex family, as her work as a graphic designer was only part-time, so this extra money was a bonus, and she adored the family.

Sarah whistled as she went into the bathroom next door to Katy's room to collect some towels that needed washing, then immediately went back downstairs.

Wow, that was close! Sadie breathed a sigh of relief. *I had better get out of here pronto.*

Sadie, who had beads of sweat on her podgy face, made a hasty departure, going unnoticed down the stairs two at a time.

Screeching with laughter, she made her way home clutching the precious pink bag belonging to Katy.

Hope it is burgers for tea. This bully had no conscience of stealing only minutes before, but, thought about herself. Always.

"Sneaking around has made me hungry," said Sadie, licking her lips as if eating the burger. "Yum, yum, pig's bum, cut off a slice, and we will all have some. Hahaha."

That was one of her old grandma's many sayings.

Sadie did not even feel remorse about the nasty way she had treated her grandma when she was alive. She had robbed out of her purse many times and offered to do shopping for the frail soul so she could keep the change. Her grandma knew but did not let on as she was frightened of her granddaughter and wondered how she would turn out as she got older.

If the truth be told, it was through Sadie's antics that her lovely grandma had passed away from a broken heart.

Chapter 11.
Angry River

The trio were deep in thought, as Art's idea was excellent in theory, however, when put into practice that could be another story.

"We don't have much choice," piped up Art as he absorbed the immediate surroundings. "What direction is the Forest of Shadows, as I am not too sure?" he asked hesitantly.

"North, across that way, over by the river." Silky pointed to the turbulent water.

"Just as I thought," Art commented. "Can anyone swim, as I can't?"

"Neither can I." Dominic shook his head in disbelief. "What are you going to do, then?" shouted Silky, becoming more agitated by the minute hoping he would not let anyone down. After all, he was helping them with his weaving, not his swimming; that was one thing he hated.

Art stared at Katy and hoped she would not feel embarrassed at what he knew.

Stepping forward towards the confused Katy, who sat with her head in her hands, he plucked up the courage to say, "Katy, I know you are an excellent swimmer and have won lots of awards at school, did you not?" He waited for her fiery response and didn't have to wait too long, as she exploded.

"How do you know anything about me?" she screeched, wondering where he got his information from. The weary youngster was puzzled and frowned.

"I know everything about you, as I have told you before, I am well aware of how clever you are at school, and I know you were a very loving person until your aunt died; is that correct?" Art reached to Katy whose heart ached at his last remark, then she furiously lashed out with her tongue.

"Why don't you mind yer own beeswax like I said before, Farty Arty?"

"Hoped you would know respect, young lady. Should I wash your mouth out with soap?"

Katy tried to ignore Art's remark as she knew he was right, but she did not care.

Do not know where he would find soap though, she tittered to herself, imagining herself foaming at the mouth with the bubbles.

"Sorry." Katy blushed and hoped Art would forgive her.

The girl is learning, Dominic smiled to himself, *as Agatha is with her in spirit*. Little did the monk know how nearby.

Art hummed happily as he strode forward to their quest.

"I have a plan, Katy, if you will only listen, as it is the only way we can get across the River of Anger," said Dominic.

"Why is it called that?" Katy enquired with an interested look on her now dirty face.

"As we have little sunlight at the moment, the moon is creating a stronger magnetic pull on the rivers and seas on our planet, which causes turbulence, and it goes on night and day except for the hour that the sun is out, hence the Angry River. Do you understand what I am trying to explain to you, young lady?" Dominic waited for an answer.

"Just because I'm a girl doesn't mean I'm stupid; of course I understand."

She stood with a determined stance, hands on hips, thrusting her face forward, not really knowing what he was talking about, but too proud to admit it; typical of Miss Katy.

Chuckling to himself, Dominic knew that this cocky young lady was lying.

Art moved closer to her and hoped she would take this seriously.

"Ahem, Katy." His throat felt it was closing up.

Better shift back a bit before she thumps me one on the chin, he thought and shuffled as he backed off from the young girl.

"We are going to assemble a makeshift bridge, and I want you to take it to the other side of the riverbank, but you must be aware of the dangers, so take your time."

Art smiled sweetly.

"What are we going to use for a bridge, and how can it be dangerous?" Katy's elfin-shaped face stared up to Art's big stupid clownlike grin.

He opened his long cloak of many colours and suddenly produced, out of a deep pocket, a xylophone which was extremely long and colourful.

Katy had never seen anything like it in her lifetime and was amazed at the size of it.

"Don't ask, Katy, as it was part of one of my many musical acts and I really don't have the time for explanations."

He fastened the instrument securely onto a large thick branch that overhung the river, and tugged the rope on it, making sure it was safe for the weight of Katy's body.

Her eyes were blinking nineteen to the dozen. Katy was a bundle of nerves as she chewed her fingernails

"Go on, Katy. We know you can do it, there's a good girl."

Dominic tried to encourage the nervous wreck of a girl who was shaking.

"I am not a baby," Katy said with a new-found confidence, as she felt that Dominic had spoken to her as if she was stupid, making her more determined to do what needed to be done, and not let them see that she was terrified.

Swimming to the other side of the turbulent waters was very tiring, as the currents were extraordinarily strong, and when Katy reached the muddy embankment to tether the thick rope round a large craggy rock, she felt absolutely worn out but extremely proud of herself as the weight of the musical ladder was very heavy. Her arms ached a bit as she leaned across the boulder, ready for action.

Coughing and spitting out the water she had swallowed, the saturated Katy tightened up the rope and glanced across the makeshift bridge expecting the other two, plus Silky, to cross over.

"Well, what are you waiting for, Christmas?" she hollered.

Typical, mused Art. *You can only expect that from Katy. Never mind, she has worked extremely hard.*

"You must come back over to this side of the bridge now." Art had to yell as the noise of the fast-flowing river drowned most of the sound.

"You must come to help Dominic across, as you know he is blind." Art was so tactless, and Dominic's face reddened as he reacted through embarrassment.

"I may be blind, but I can walk, so I don't need pity."

Feeling ashamed, Art replied, "Sorry, it's not pity, it is the river; it is causing the bridge to sway and shake, so we must be here for each other, as Katy might not be able to find her own balance, so I will hold it at this end while you both cross over, then I will follow when you reach the other side as one of you can hold it steady.

That went down a bit better with Dominic as he apologised for being too touchy.

Blind? Young Katy had good intuition and knew that something was wrong with Dominic, but not blindness.

"Well, I never did," the weary Katy growled. *But there again, I did wonder why he was a bit unsteady on his feet. I thought he was just a doddery old fool!* She giggled to herself. *Aw, bless him. I must be going soft.* Katy felt compassion for the monk.

"I will stay over this side until you are both over safely."

Art helped Dominic towards the edge of the completed bridge. Each of the colourful aluminium slats, eight in all, represented one musical note, a musical octave. "You can come over now, madam," screeched Art above the roar of the Angry River.

As Katy stepped onto the first coloured slat of the instrument, her feet started to take on a life of their own. Tap, tap, she felt as if her feet were tingling. There to her amazement were circles of multicoloured lights, full of magic and power.

Dancing around her ankles, this energy force propelled her across the different notes of the musical bridge.

"Do re me fa so la ti doh." Katy was exhilarated and had never danced so well since her aunt had passed away.

"Oh, Aunt Agatha, if only you could see me now," she sighed sadly.

Little did she know that her elderly aunt was watching her from the cave of Magi, the oracle-reader, not more than a hundred miles away.

"You are a good friend to rescue me, Magi, and I will always be in your debt." Agatha was so grateful to this dear friend she had come to know.

"I saw lovely angels on my journey up to the spirit world, and just as I felt that something was not quite right, you stepped in, Magi, so what are you hiding from me, I wonder?"

Agatha searched his lived-in old face with the brown sparkling eyes for an answer.

"Do not worry, lass, just use the crystal anytime you want, to keep your eye on your niece. Think of it as having a neighbourhood watch."

"Well, if you say so, thanks." Agatha turned her attention back to the round shiny orb after wiping more dust off it.

She was impressed at what she saw. "That's my girl! I knew you could do it; nice work."

Agatha wiped a tear away as she continued to watch her great niece's progress.

"This plucky madam has no idea that I am tuning into her whereabouts, watching everything that she does, but this is a learning process for her, and I am here to help every step of the way where possible."

Magi stroked his untidy long grey beard, nodding his head in agreement.

Chapter 12.
Reported Missing

"Where can she be, David? It has been more than twenty-four hours since Katy's disappearance. Oh God, what can we do? She might be lying dead somewhere. Please, somebody out there, help us to find our precious daughter, please." Nat sobbed. "Listen, sweetheart, it has taken something like this for us to realise just how much we love her and I'm sure we will be given the chance to tell her and also pay her more attention. bless her." David tried his best to comfort his wife but was not sure about them finding his younger daughter and did not want to worry his distraught wife with his negative thoughts.

"The police are doing all they can, Nat, and like we said before, it could be Katy getting up to her old tricks and playing silly games."

David needed to reassure Nat constantly, so he crossed his fingers and prayed.

Dione and James were so wrapped up in their school prom that they did not give a second thought to their younger sister's fate.

"Have I got too much hair gel on, Mum, and is it spiky enough?"

James swaggered into her bedroom obviously dressed up for his big debut, his mind thinking about the girl he may be paired up with for the evening.

"If I do not like her, I can always dump her and find some other chick."

He caught sight of himself in the mirror and straightened his tie.

"Mum, do you realise how handsome your son is?" he said and winked.

Nat had to chuckle to herself as James was a good-looking lad and he had a brilliant personality and lots of confidence, which is why he was popular at school. "You gorgeous hunk of a son! Give me a hug and off you go before you are late."

Beaming with pride, Nat held James tightly knowing that he was growing up fast. *I hope Katy is safe as I would give anything to be hugging my young problem child,* thought Nat.

"We believe that you knew Katy Bex but did not get on with her, did you?" The policeman had a profoundly serious face.

Inspector Linley studied Sadie Frost's 'think I am bothered' attitude, and he knew straight away that she was trouble.

"Course I knew her. I went to school with her, didn't I?"

The girl could not look at the policeman but played around with a red hairband that she was holding.

"Don't get cocky with me, young lady, as we may lock you up for obstructing the course of justice."

He was only pretending, as she was too young to be locked up; however, Sadie was not aware of this.

The Inspector sensed that this girl was guilty of something, as she was on the defence straight away.

He gazed at her with his steel-grey eyes hoping to unnerve her, but she was as tough as they come, or so she thought.

"We heard a rumour that you pinched young Katy Bex's mobile phone; is that correct?"

"Are you asking me or telling me?" Sadie mocked the Inspector.

"Anyway, I ain't got no mobile, so if it's a rumour, prove it."

Sadie turned quite pale as she tried to keep her cool but she knew she was losing it.

"I promise you this, young lady, we will be back, so think about it and think hard, ok?"

The Inspector smiled calmly as Sadie made a hasty retreat up the stairs.

"Good day, Mrs Frost; we will be back." He nodded confidently as he walked outside.

Sadie's mother wrung her hands together and wondered what her handful of a daughter had got herself into this time; it was not the first time she had been in trouble with the police. Sadie was beside herself with worry and did not know which way to turn which was very unusual for her.

Coming back down the stairs slowly, she said hesitantly, "Mum, I bet that flipping Danny Jones has put the blame on me. He is the one who's got her stupid phone, so, wait till I get my hands on him; he will be so sorry."

She chewed her fingernails as her crafty mind planned the next move.

"Why don't you tell the police then, my girl? It would soon clear this matter up instead of putting me through this."

"Listen, Mum, just leave it. I'll sort him out."

Sadie knew she had to keep quiet, as she had pinched the bag, of which nothing had been mentioned. Best leave the bully boy alone as he seemed to have a habit of knowing what Sadie was up to. She was sure Danny Jones watched every move she made so she could not be too careful.

Katy's pink bag was tucked well out of the way and no one knew it was missing as yet. Anyway, some of the emails in it were alien to Sadie.

"Magi, Keeper of dreams@cloud.air? What's all that about? It's flippin' all Chinese to me." Sadie became irritated as she thumbed the book and thought it only fit for the bin. "What if I get rid of it? Knowing my luck, they will find it, then I will be in big trouble. No, better keep it hidden out of sight," she sighed and wondered if it was worth the hassle. She tried to stuff it under the broken floorboards in her bedroom.

"Get in, you pain in the backside." it was a tight squeeze, but after pushing and shoving, she managed to hide the bag and its contents well out of the way.

"Phew, glad that's sorted." Sadie was so relieved that she gave a sigh of relief and left the bedroom, closing the door behind her. "Wonder what Mother is going to say about this. I hope she does not keep rambling on about me and my devious ways as I am in no mood for earache." Charming!!

Her mother did not know half of what was going on, otherwise, she would have gone ballistic, and then made contact with Inspector Linley immediately to get Sadie to confess.

Chapter 13.
Wind and Huccanites

The trio plodded on as Katy, wet, bedraggled and dirty, was trailing behind now as she was tired and hungry. "I haven't eaten since I got to this horrible place, and I would give anything for a big cream doughnut. Yum!" She licked her lips as her tummy rumbled constantly. She had hunger pains but tried to ignore her problem and concentrate on the surroundings instead. Suddenly, they stumbled across a small copse with sapling trees and flowers growing in abundance.

Strange, thought Katy, *without a lot of sunshine you would think the colourful display would not survive, hmm.*

"These are moon blossoms and they have magical qualities," Art whispered as if it was a secret.

Pointing to lovely dark blue feather-like plants, Dominic explained, "We drink nectar from the plants which is a potion for energy and a bite to eat." He had read her mind. "With what, fresh air?" Katy retorted angrily, thinking that the old monk had gone doolally tap (crackers). She rubbed the blisters on her feet that had developed over the last few days.

"Huh, I've heard it all now," his female friend muttered as she swallowed the golden liquid.

"Wow, it tastes absolutely delicious and it makes my nose tingle." Katy sneezed as she drank from a leaf.

"Yum! Can I have some more, please?" "Yes, my dear." Dominic smiled as he gave the much happier child the nourishing nectar.

She hastily finished her second helping.

Silky had set off a good couple of hours earlier, full of excitement, weaving his silken thread in and out of shrubs, rocks, trees and undergrowth with great enthusiasm, knowing that he would be helping the Keeper of Dreams and all the unhappy souls too, as hopefully, the sunlight would be restored to this dark planet, enabling them all to be healed.

"Sing, Katy; we cannot hear you."

Art was trying to encourage her along the dark landscape as they trudged over hill and dale. "If I sing any louder I will damage my throat," she screeched.

"What about my ears?" Art yelled.

"You're doing fine," added Dominic. "Just sing a note higher - that will be excellent, Katy, believe me, as it lifts the planet's vibrations to a higher level of love and harmony."

"Whatever." *Load of rubbish* she thought and laughed at him quietly so as not to offend. *Not like me at all,* she thought.

I cannot do anything right, the stroppy little Madam thought. *Well, I will show them.*

This is just what Dominic wanted.

Katy's voice became crystal clear and as they approached the Forest of Shadows, a heaviness was felt on their shoulders and they noticed that the spider's web was no longer shimmering or vibrating. They looked at each other and there, in the centre of bracken and shrubs, lay the broken body of Silky, the beautiful creature who had brought them this far. He had risked his own life for them.

Crying with anguish, Katy picked Silky up and dusted the leaves from his wonderful long lashes and tried to rub some life back into him, but it was too late. Poor Silky. They were devastated, and Art had lost his best friend ever.

Woosh!

What was this change in the air that they all sensed which brought a fierce gust of wind that sucked the earth into the air like a tornado?

Katy cowered while trying to huddle up closer to Dominic.

Wooosh! The white smoky apparition hovered above the trio as if it was enfolding them into its arms.

"I am the Wind Whisperer; do not worry as I am here to protect you."

The shining form began to manifest into a long flowing wide funnel, with slanted green eyes and a wonderfully happy smiley face. His body radiated a beautiful light.

As the group got over the shock of this, they noticed a loud rumbling noise in the distance.

Katy reached out and Dominic held her hand tightly.

"We will be ok if we stay positive, my child." She whimpered, "Do you really think so? I am so frightened."

Suddenly, there was a thundering of hooves being driven faster and faster.

Approaching the terrified trio, the black horses encircled them. The riders, the Huccanites, waved swords above their heads, swinging them as they rode round and round in circles.

There seemed to be no way out until the Wind Whisperer proceeded to blow with all his might.

His chest expanded full of air that he had sucked in, and as he expelled it, the force of it knocked the Huccanites out of their rhythm of speed, off their horses' backs and they were falling down like skittles at a bowling alley.

The three of them huddled together in a circle, their arms around each other for protection.

Katy knew that there was imminent danger and hung on for dear life. They had killed their best friend and she was gutted. How could a vulnerable little spider have fought back? He did not stand a chance with these aggressive killers.

As the hunters lay winded, one of them whined, "Keep away from Marble Mountain or you will be doomed."

"What do they mean?" The tired child was puzzled by the outburst from these evil warriors, and she shook with fear.

"My dear child, their great leader, Hucan enslaves souls who were making their way here to the Planet of Light. The poor souls were very ill when they passed away on Earth and needed to be healed in the Halls of Healing which is here on our Planet of Light, but we are losing that light rapidly."

Wind Whisperer wrapped himself around the group as he tried to explain further.

"Hucan intercepts their journey to this planet and keeps them as slaves."

His voice suddenly changed as he whispered, "Hang on for your life."

He began to spin so fast around the area of dry ground that he created a tunnel-shaped vortex, which lifted the Huccanites upwards into the air, spinning them round and round, then they were dumped like a ton of bricks onto the hardened earth.

They were thrown about like rag dolls, falling and bumping themselves on the hard rocks which jutted out of the earth.

They staggered around blindly, searching for their swords that were strewn all over, buckled and broken. When they stopped feeling dizzy, they ran so fast you could not see them for dust.

Unfortunately for them, the horses had bolted as quickly as possible away from the destruction of the Wind Whisperer.

The onlookers roared with laughter, the tears streaming down their faces as the Huccanites ran like the clappers.

The calm which descended upon them all was mind-blowing. "Ha, ha, not wind-blowing!" Katy and her silly sense of humour.

"Ah, they are not so brave now," giggled a very relieved young lady.

"Thank you, Wind Whisperer; you have saved our lives and we will always be grateful. God bless you." Dominic bowed to the airy ethereal white figure, who had risen higher into the darkness and waved his cloak-like form to them as he ascended into the night sky.

"Goodbye, and good luck to you all." Woosh! He was gone.

There were tears in Katy's eyes and she wiped them away quickly as she did not want her friends to think that she was showing a softer side to her normal angry nature.

Stupid girl, she told herself and dusted off all the bits of flying debris, leaves, bracken and earth that had stuck to her as they had also become part of the spinning tunnel of wind, albeit more on the outer edge where it was safer.

At least they had been protected and were now out of danger; well, for the time being anyway.

"I am blooming knackered." Katy rubbed her eyes and yawned wearily as she felt that she would just drop.

"Tired, you mean tired." Art corrected her as he also knew that they all needed a good night's sleep.

"Hmm, just like having my dad around." Katy shook her head.

"Ok, let's find somewhere safe for the night."

"And comfortable," mumbled the confused child. Katy wanted a cuddle as she was so lonely. However, she kept her mouth shut and wrapped her pink pyjamas tightly around herself.

I miss Aunt Agatha so much; she gave me plenty of hugs and cuddles.

Her thoughts were very much on her family, back home on Mother Earth, and of how much she missed them, but also the guilt as to how she treated them all. *They must hate me.*

She felt pain in her heart, which was unusual for Katy, and losing their beautiful friend Silky, who had sacrificed his life for them, was also devastating for her.

Those Huccanites have got a lot to answer for.

It just dawned on Katy that she had lost some of her magical powers since coming to the Planet of Light.

Shame, I would have made mincemeat out of them and turned them into sausages, but I bet they would not taste nice. Yuk! Katy felt sick at the thought of it.

Chapter 14.
The Will

Meanwhile, in a small village in England, there was a plan unfolding which would bring chaos to the Bex Family.

The young man, who appeared to be in his thirties, scrutinised the newspaper left behind by someone in the betting shop.

He was dirty, needed a shave and a change of clothing and seemed to have been living rough for a while.

Searching through the well-read paper, he came across a photograph of a school proms gathering with all the pictures of the teenagers, their names included.

"Mmm…" His eyes lit up with excitement as he spoke out loud. "Dione and James Bex, from Higham Comprehensive School. Well, I never; that is very interesting."

Richard rubbed his unshaven chin with the cuff of the filthy jacket as he looked closer.

I recognise the likeness to Aunt Agatha. Yes! I have cracked it.

Jumping up and down with joy, he fished in the pocket of his grubby bomber jacket and produced a dirty old road map, tattered and torn, but still readable.

Sitting on the red plastic chair in the betting shop, he marked his journey out and realised it was within ten minutes walking distance to Higham where they lived.

Ding a Ling! The bell on the door of the post office tinkled as Richard Bex pushed his way past an elderly customer who was coming out of the shop.

"Excuse me is the word, young man. Where's your manners?" The frail old gentleman swayed as he regained balance on his arthritic legs.

The arrogant Richard ignored him as he had other things on his mind, important things.

"I am looking for the Bex family; have you heard of them?" he asked the old shop assistant curtly.

"The Bex family? Of course! Everyone knows them around here. Are you visiting?" the postmistress asked, happy to help this unkempt figure.

"Unfortunately, their Aunt Agatha died suddenly many months ago. Such a shame as she was well-loved by us all. She was such charming lady."

"But where do they live?" demanded Richard, who was becoming impatient, and was not really interested in Agatha having passed away.

"Up the hill to the right, first left, then straight ahead, up the long gravel driveway and you cannot miss it," the shop assistant said, pointing out directions.

"C'mon, woman; the name of the place will do."

"Maple Manor," she retorted. The postmistress was not impressed with this ignorant young man and was glad to see the back of him. He pushed his way out past the other customers as if he did not have a minute to spare.

"God, it's some trek up this hill," panted Richard. "I hope it's blooming worth it."

Eventually, he reached the main wrought iron gates and made his way hastily along the grey gravel path.

"Could have done with a lift up here." He was flagging a bit now and could not wait to see what reception he would receive. Laughing heartily, he approached an old wooden oak door.

Ringing the large brass bell that dangled on an old chain, he hopped about from one foot to the other; patience was something he did not have.

"Is anyone at home?" he shouted with gusto. "Hello there, is anybody in? Speak up now for goodness' sake, I haven't got all day."

Sarah, the young domestic, was coming round the side of the house when she spotted him.

"Can I help you, Sir?" The happy friendly girl was very polite and waited for a response from this seedy-looking character. *Ugh! He gives me the creeps.* Sarah felt her flesh crawl and tried not to stare at him.

"Who are you, eh? The lady of the house or a poor servant?" Richard sneered at her.

"More to the point, who are you? And how dare you speak like that to me! We are in the twenty-first century, not the dark ages, you horrible man."

Sarah nearly called him a gentleman; a big mistake - he was anything but.

"Listen, little maid in waiting, I would be careful if I were you. You may find yourself out of a job when I take over." He smiled at his last remark.

"Take over! Take over?! What are you going on about, and who are you anyway?"

Sarah was frantic by now and her voice grew louder.

"Is there something wrong?" Nat had heard the raised voices and had hurried out of the hallway towards the duo.

"Mrs Bex, th-this is…" The young lady shook with fear, as this horror was towering over her in a very menacing way.

Richard swept Sarah aside and held out his grubby hands towards Nat.

"Pleased to meet you, Mrs Bex," the arrogant upstart announced with attitude.

"Who am I talking to?" Nat snapped, as she did not like the look of him.

"Richard, Richard Bex. Pleased to meet you, my dear."

Baffled by his reply, Nat clutched her hands tightly, as she did not want to touch his grubby fingers.

She felt that there was something sinister about this man, who was waiting to shake her hand.

How could he be related? She could not believe it, as David did not have any other living relatives besides herself and the children.

Explain yourself, Mr Bex!" she exclaimed abruptly.

"Will I give it to you straight, lady?" He smiled in a sickly way as he stared at the curious looks he was getting.

"This house, this mansion, is mine and everything that goes with it belongs to me, and I've got proof in black and white." He had to refrain from laughing at the shock on both their faces.

"Well, what have you got to say about that then, Mrs stuck-up Madam?" He sneered as he spoke, and as quick as a flash, he pulled a piece of dirty rolled up paper out of his even dirtier pocket.

"This here is your aunt's Last Will and Testimony."

He smugly waved it under their noses.

"Testament; you mean testament." Nat started to panic and felt quite sick at the thought of the Will that they knew nothing about, and of this jumped-up arrogant person who surely was not a relative.

It must be true. Her mind was all over the place now wondering where to turn to.

"Sarah, please phone David. He must be on his way home by now. Quickly, there's a good girl."

Running as far away from this cruel ill-mannered person, Nat ran towards the long drive and was relieved at the sound of a car that was coming up the drive.

There was a sharp screech of brakes as David turned into the drive. He dived out of the driving seat and ran towards his distraught wife, wondering what the problem was.

Turning round, he saw the scruffy effigy in front of him and stared earnestly into the venomous eyes which were filled with hate.

Both men would become enemies, of course.

"Your name, sir, is?" David did not have to ask a second time.

"Richard Bex, the adopted son of Agatha Bex, deceased, I may add."

As if they didn't already know that.

"And, as I have already informed your missus here, I am in receipt of my mother's Last Will and Testament." He waved the yellow parchment under David's nose.

David felt as if the bottom had dropped out of his world; what with Katy missing and now this, he had to remain calm.

"Let us all go inside, shall we? And try to be civilised about this."

His stomach was all churned up as he led this stranger through to the farmhouse kitchen.

The three of them gathered around the kitchen table while Sarah made them all a drink.

The scruffy intruder opened out the now very frayed document for them all to see.

"Now, what does that say?" he asked sarcastically as he pointed to the document, which was grubby.

He was becoming very impatient. All he wanted was to get his hands on this great fortune as soon as possible.

The letters stood out boldly.

THE LAST WILL AND TESTAMENT OF AGATHA BEX

Dated 16/11/1994

I, AGATHA BEX, BEQUEATH ALL MY MONIES AND ESTATE TO MY ADOPTED SON:

RICHARD THOMAS BEX.

IN THE EVENT OF HIS DEATH, I BEQUEATH THE ABOVE-MENTIONED TO DAVID BEX, MY NEPHEW.

WITNESSED BY MACHU AGONGA

Aunt Agatha and Machu had both signed this legal document.

There were gasps of shock and horror when the once-happy couple read the Will. The bottom of their world had just dropped out.

"Aunt Agatha didn't have much money then, and she never mentioned an adopted son."

Nat spat the words out in anger, feeling insecure for her family's future.

She collapsed into the nearest chair with tears streaming down her face.

"What will become of us?" she wailed as she hung onto David, who was deep in thought.

"Now, now, stop this nonsense, there has obviously been a mistake, so we will see a solicitor as soon as."

He tried to comfort his distressed wife as he put his arms around her, noticing the grin on the stranger's face, who was taking the stained paperwork off the table.

With a glint of smugness, he put the Will back into his pocket, shouting as he left, "See you in court." His evil laugh lingered for some time after he was gone.

If only the Bex family knew how this scumbag had treated their aunt; they would be appalled at the violent abuse, both mentally and physically, that this beast had put her through.

No wonder Aunt Agatha had pushed it all to the back of her mind, not wanting to be reminded of it, as it was all too painful.

If only Agatha had told them all about it, it would have saved them from this terrible trail of worry that may destroy them, leaving them with nothing.

Nat could still hear the laughter of the villain ringing in her ears. She shivered as she prayed for help.

"What is going on, Mum? Has somebody upset you?

Only I have just seen a dirty tramp scarpering down the drive, and he stunk foul." James was out of breath as he checked that his mum was ok.

He ran his hands through his hair which was, by now, all over the place. Putting it in place, he scowled and clenched his fist in anger as his mum explained what had happened. "I will sort him out. Just wait and see."

Mrs Banks had come on the scene after all the noise that had been going on. Wiping her floury hands on her apron, she reached out to the irate James.

"Calm yourself down, son; whatever it is, it isn't worth shouting about, is it? Just as I was finishing off baking a lovely apple pie. Now, come on, it is not the end of the world, is it?"

The cook waited for a reply from a very flushed James.

David, who was seething at this point, stepped in front of James.

145

"You could not be further away from the truth, Mrs Banks. Anyway, put the kettle on and we will tell you all about it as it could affect your job here."

"My job? Oh no! What have I done wrong?"

Fumbling for another tissue, Nat wiped her tears away, helping the now upset Mrs Banks to a chair.

"We have enough to worry about with Katy missing for the last few days without all this on top of it, God help us."

"Well, I think the house has been nice and quiet with smelly Katy gone," James piped up as he sipped his cup of tea and helped himself to another piece of apple pie, calm now, as if everything were normal.

Dione, who had just walked into the kitchen, had heard his remark and was livid.

She belted James across the back of his head.

"Get off, you ugly cow." Jumping up, he tried to hit out at his sister, but David managed to grab him back in time

"Pack it in, the pair of you, or else you will both be grounded for a week."

"Huh! Grounded at my age! I'm not a kid anymore," James complained, not noticing the water on the kitchen floor. He slipped and fell, knocking his nose on the stone floor.

"Serves you right," Dione sniggered.

"Dad, tell her to stop laughing at me." His face was red with anger and embarrassment as he picked himself up from the floor. "That was actually sore and not to be laughed at; so rude, Dione." The fifteen-year-old was fuming.

"Act like a child and you will be treated like one."

"Go on; get up those stairs both of you, now."

"But Dad…" Dione smiled trying to get round her father.

"None of your backchat, girl."

"We need to stick together in situations like this, not argue with one another. I'm disgusted with you both."

James and Dione looked silently at their parents and sulked up the stairs, both ashamed that they had let them down badly.

"Wonder where smelly Katy has gone, though." Looking at each other, they both knew that they missed their little sister so much and the house was soulless without her.

I bet, wherever she is, she will be causing trouble," James moaned. He missed her really.

Chapter 15.
Marble Mountain

"Wow, look! It's flipping wicked! See how it shines in the moonlight."

Katy was pointing to a mountain in the distance, and it was surrounded by a wonderful warm orange glow.

Wondering what it was, the trio quickened their step towards this strange place, hoping that they would also find a place of rest.

Eventually, they found themselves following a pathway that was lit up by hundreds of tiny pebbles scattered along the way. It was very rough to walk on but there was no other road that would lead them there.

The coloured pebbles were made of glass and seemed to be laid on a lane of light that shone through showing them the way.

As they slowly moved along the path, they suddenly came within twenty yards of an entrance that resembled a highly polished disc of gold, shimmering in the darkness on the mountainside.

It was all very inviting to unsuspecting visitors who knew nothing about the dark secrets which the mountain held.

They did not realise it was Marble Mountain.

As they approached the closed doorway, they could feel tingling in their foreheads. They were all confused and looked very concerned.

Dominic frowned as he felt that there was some force of evil here, and in his mind, he visualised a bright white light wrapping itself around him and his friends to protect them, hoping it would act as a shield bouncing any evil back to where it came from.

Feeling more confident now, the three of them moved closer to the entrance.

Immediately, there was a sound in the distance which became louder and louder.

Sounding like a bell tolling, it was a strange tone, and, all at once, the gold circular doorway opened allowing them to enter, which they did. They had to find Grabb, the Jackdaw and the Emerald Key even though they could be facing great danger.

There was a droning sound that filled their heads as it was trying to bring their mind body and spirit under control, and it began to make them feel sick and disorientated.

Panic filled them now.

Dominic stepped in; "Now listen, we must act fast as danger lies ahead due to the droning noise, so, to stop it happening, use the white light quickly. It will protect us; do it now."

There was urgency in Dominic's voice as he crossed himself and said his prayers for them all.

Eventually, the noise seemed to weaken as the white light kicked in.

They were all relieved and were curious to find out what this strange place was all about.

Katy was placing her feet carefully as she walked across the rough green pebbles, when she noticed a large pool of water, so dark that you could not see down into the bottom of it.

They all stood in amazement for, surrounding the water, there were angelic-like figures radiating the most beautiful colours you could imagine.

There was also rainbow-coloured water cascading over the ethereal beings into the dark pond, but it dispelled immediately on hitting the dark water.

Art was in awe of this and was also so hypnotised by the wonderful musical sounds coming from their angelic faces that he forgot about visualising the bright light for protection. He ventured further to the edge of the swirling mass that engrossed all that surrounded it.

Keeping her distance, Katy sat herself on a dark crescent-shaped stone which nearly surrounded the black circle of water. She wondered what was in store for them as she had a bad feeling of doom and gloom.

Following her, Art dropped down beside her. He was very tired and thirsty and as he reached towards the pool to sip some water, out jumped a strange ugly-looking wide-mouthed fish.

It had large spiky teeth and an evil grin on its face. *Hmm, an early lunch.* He licked his massive lips in anticipation.

Snap! The fish grabbed Art, who was not quick enough to get out of the way, and it dragged his thrashing body down into the murky depths of the now turbulent water, then let go of him. *I will have my snack later, yummy, after I find some greens to go with him.* Off he swam.

"Help me! Help me!" Art felt that all was lost as he was thrown like a bundle of rags into a corner of a cave-like structure, which was filled with all sorts of pathetic beings who filled Art's heart with horror and sadness.

As Art composed himself, he weighed everybody up.

They appeared to be so lost and bewildered that Art decided he had to help them all escape from this foul-smelling hellhole.

They were all trapped in this cave below water, but there was at least some air in it to keep them alive even though it smelled rotten, just like fish.

"Art, Art, where are you?" Katy was very frightened as Art had not surfaced from the black watery mass. He had been down there awhile she thought as Dominic looked troubled about what had happened.

"Come on, Katy, run." Dominic was in a state of panic knowing that their lives could be in danger, but he knew that Art would find a way to escape these evil people.

The blind monk reached out to where he sensed Katy was and dragged her away from the side of the black pool.

"Oi! You nearly pulled my arm out of its socket, Dominic, you silly burke."

Running towards a faint light in the distance while tightly holding Katy's hand, Dominic wondered where Grabb the Jackdaw had flown to.

He quickened his pace and ignored the young girl's moaning. They had to get out of this place and find the Emerald Key.

Chapter 16.
Forest of Shadows

Tweet, tweet, tweet. Grabb the Jackdaw preened his wings as he settled comfortably in his newly made home of moss leaves and dried twigs high up in the treetops.

The Emerald Key glistened in the light of the moon and Grabb knew that he had to be incredibly careful in hiding it, as anyone could steal it. After all, it appeared to be very precious.

After he covered it up carefully amongst the leaves, he decided to go off searching for worms as he was rather hungry.

His tummy rumbled as he felt the pangs of hunger.

Grabb had been flying for ages, and he was so tired he could hardly keep his eyes open.

Could do with a kip never mind dinner, but my stomach feels as if my throat has been cut.

Up and down, he soared, in between the many trees of the Forest of Shadows, unaware of the brown beady eyes spying on him from a distance.

Minkey, the brown woolly monkey, wondered why Grabb had taken so long to make his nest and swiftly climbed the gnarled old oak tree to investigate his hunch. The coast was clear while Grabb was off looking for some dinner.

He threw the contents of the nest onto the forest floor and quickly dropped down through the branches to inspect the bounty that he had come across.

"What have we got here, then? Very nice, very precious."

Minkey examined the green Emerald Key which was set in gold, hanging from a golden chain, and it dawned on him that it was worth a fortune.

"Yippee! I am going to be rich, rich enough to escape from this dark planet!" He jumped up and down with excitement.

He scratched his lumpy head thinking *Hucan will let me escape to another Planet of Light for this.*

The cunning monkey knew that the cruel leader of the Huccanites would do anything to gain possession of this treasure which held powers that Minkey did not know of. He was becoming more excitable not realising that once the key was in Hucan's hands, there would never be a chance of light or healing for all the sick souls on this planet. Wrapping up the treasure in a dock leaf, Minkey made sure it was safely attached to him by a piece of twine bound tightly around his leg.

He quickly made his way through the deep canopy of the forest, swinging from one tree to the next.

"Marble Mountain, here I come!" This was Hucan's home.

Bouncing up and down with glee, Minkey moved faster along the rough pebble path which felt as if it was cutting the skin on his tiny feet.

"It is worth a few cuts and scrapes that won't harm me. Ouch."

He hobbled speedily onwards towards Marble Mountain.

On hearing a noise, Minkey froze to the spot as a large shadow appeared in front of the monkey, and as he looked towards it, he recognised one of the Huccanite soldiers.

"Who goes there? Show yourself or you will be destroyed immediately."

The stern-faced soldier moved closer to have a good look at this woolly creature who was, by now, shaking like a leaf.

"I …I am hoping to see your leader as I have something special, in fact, precious, for him."

Minkey was quivering as he grovelled to the evil soldier.

"Precious? Precious? What would you know about precious?" snarled the Huccanite as he dragged the terrified monkey along the ground towards Marble Mountain.

Aunt Agatha was watching all this through the magic glass.

She snapped her fingers and Magi jumped to attention.

"Spell book, pronto! The Emerald Key is within reach if only we can do something to save it."

Out came the Izzy Wizzy Bible again.

"Strut yer stuff, Magi." Agatha stood back as Magi stuck out his chest looking ever so important.

Thumbing through his special magic book, he found what he was looking for. He proceeded to chant his spell with wand in hand.

"Send us help to clear the way,
Emerald Key is here to stay.
Send a stallion or a steed,
any colour, any creed.
Save the monkey and the key,
we need help immediately."

Zamoosh! There was a massive ball of bright purple smoke hanging in the air as Magi's spell was activated.

Cough! Splutter! Magi was thrown backwards as his wand that wielded the power was ripped out of his hand with the force of the energy that created the magic.

Composing himself, he straightened his black cape and his orange pointed hat, then retrieved his dusty wand from the corner of his cave, so glad that it was not broken.

"That is worth a drink at least, Aggie. What do you say to that?"

"Cheers, big ears!" She laughed as she put the kettle on for some home-brewed lunar tea.

"Ha, ha, he does have big ears," she whispered to herself, wondering how long it would take for the spell to work. They both peered into the glass oracle.

There was a bright flash that blinded the Huccanite.

Taken by surprise, he dropped Minkey and out of the shadows appeared a white unicorn standing proud. Its antenna-like horn had picked up the spell from Magi. Prancing towards Minkey, she shouted, "I am Purity, your guardian angel. I move as fast as light.

Jump on my back; hurry up, we haven't got all day, as these soldiers will destroy you and your treasure. Trust no one. We need to make our way to the crystal caves immediately."

"What is that about, clever clogs? You could be after the valuables, so why should I trust you?" Minkey was angry. "Well, make your mind up; are you coming or not, matey?" The terrified monkey had no choice as he pounced onto Purity's back, tightly grasping her neck as she glided swiftly across the barren wilderness, making her way towards the Crystal Cave which was a long way off.

"I know the planet is in trouble and time is running out for all of us," Purity said gently, "and I hope we reach the Crystal Cave in time to save us all. You, Minkey, have the answer with the Emerald Key, so hang onto your hollyhocks and off we go."

Purity's lithe body rose up into the dark sky as she moved faster and faster towards their goal, and Minkey hung on for dear life, unaware of a pathetic bunch of souls not too far away, who had to find their freedom quickly before they perished under Hucan's rule. Little did he know that their paths would entwine.

Chapter 17.
Lost Souls

"C'mon, wake up and smell the coffee! Are you all giving up without a fight?" "Coffee? Yes please, two sugars," came a voice from the back of the cave, as they all laughed.

As Art settled down, he puffed out his chest and cockily looked around, eying up these forlorn creatures.

There were tiny fairies with broken wings as well as their spirits. There were the old and the young with all sorts of illnesses, from broken bones to bad hearts, and babies who just wanted a cuddle and a sleep in a warm place with food in their tummies. Some had limbs missing. The sight pulled on Art's heartstrings.

One figure hobbled to the front of the cave and his clothes were like strips of rags that were clinging onto his bent body. He looked about ten years of age but had the body of an old man.

Approaching Art hesitantly, he swallowed hard to pluck up the courage and the energy to speak.

"What makes you think we can get out of here? You don't know what's going on, do you, coming here and telling us all to be strong?"

The youngster was becoming very agitated but knew that he had to get his point of view over for him and his friends.

"You ain't got a clue, mate. Have you heard of Hucan, the leader of the Huccanites?"

Tears were rolling down the battered and bruised face of this frail body as he sobbed.

"I have seen them," Art replied. "But we had a lucky escape through some entity called the Wind Whisperer, so yes, my friend, I have met the Huccanites, but not their leader and I am not willing to give into them."

The forlorn figure was eager to tell this clown-like gentleman their story to make him realize why they were so petrified of Hucan and his platoon of soldiers.

"Are you sitting comfortably? Well, I will begin."

Art was staring earnestly at the ten-year-old as he waited on the story unfolding.

Meanwhile, above water level, Dominic had pulled Katy along as she struggled to go back to rescue Art.

As they were approaching the distant light, Dominic was still trying to convince the heartbroken young girl that they had to flee.

"My girl, it is too dangerous. We have been tricked by Hucan. Look at the way those angelic beings surrounding the pool changed into Huccanite warriors, and all it took was a blink of an eye.

"We must not waste any more time worrying about our good friend Art's welfare, as we owe it to the rest of the souls on the planet to find the Emerald Key, and if I know Art, he will survive."

Little did they know that the treasure had been stolen from Grabb the Jackdaw and had nearly ended up in the hands of Hucan.

Chapter 18.
Magi's Oracle

Aunt Agatha was watching from afar as usual and could see the Huccanites following the unsuspecting pair.

Her great-niece, Katy, and the monk were now running in fear for their lives.

"Oh, Magi, do something, hurry up, you slowcoach."

"Do you want me to help you or are you going to continue insulting me?"

Magi was becoming more annoyed as Agatha was bossing him around now.

"Sorry, Magi, it's just that I am so stressed with the fear of something happening to Katy."

"That's no excuse for being rude, now, is it?" Magi waited for a reply from the old lady who was ashamed of her behaviour to her good friend and he was so right.

"Forgive me, please, Magi."

He accepted the apology and quickly opened his Izzy Wizzy Bible.

"Let me see." He blew stardust from the golden bound cover of his ancient manual, searching through it hastily, searching for yet another spell to save Katy and her friend.

Running towards the entrance at the end of the cavernous tunnel, the weary pair saw a trickle of water leading to the outside of the mountain.

There was a shaft of moonlight shining on it making it sparkle and lighting up their only escape route.

As they stepped outside, the trickle became a raging ocean as the Huccanites released hundreds of gallons of shark-infested water, which had been collected in a dam-like structure.

"Magi, Magi!" Agatha tore at her frizzy hair in despair, begging the wizard for help.

"Izzy Wizzy Bible, do your thing,
Change the sharks to sweet dolphins.
Make the oceans quieten down,
Take them to safe solid ground."

Agatha knew that Magi would come to the rescue as always and she was over the moon, so to speak.

A massive blue wave came crashing down over the hungry sharks and they were so taken by surprise when they suddenly changed into two beautiful dolphins.

Dominic sat down and cried.

"No time for tears! Jump on our backs and we will take you on a ride that you will never forget."

The leader of the dolphins beckoned the couple who were very wary now of everything and everybody.

They both looked at each other with the same thoughts of how Art was going to make a miraculous escape from Marble Mountain and where their own journey was going to take them.

They held hands which felt comforting.

The forlorn figure was eager to tell Art their story to make him realise why they were all so frightened of the evil leader, Hucan.

"When we, all of us here..." Ben was becoming more and more anxious, and Art touched his hand gently, saying, "Take your time, son, I am listening."

"Well, when we were alive, or should I say in our Earth bodies, we were on a Help the Environment Day."

"Doing what?" Art was extremely interested.

"Cleaning all the rubbish along the sides of the canals and planting trees. As you know, the trees filter the polluted air and give out clean air so that we can all breathe in oxygen that keeps us alive."

"Yes, it certainly does, so what went wrong?"

Art was eager to know and was becoming impatient as he tapped his foot rapidly against a big rock.

"We were working near a bridge that spanned the canal and there was an oil tanker travelling across the bridge. "The driver lost control while on his mobile phone instead of keeping his eyes on the road.

The tanker careered off the road, through the walls of the bridge and landed onto the canal side where we were working and as you can see, we all have different injuries and did not manage to survive the accident.

The lucky driver survived but has to live with the guilt for the rest of his life, so I suppose he has suffered also."

"But what has that got to do with Hucan, eh, Ben?"

Ben was finding it difficult as he was reliving the terror again and gave a big sigh. His shoulders dropped in despair.

Art's mind wandered, thinking about Dominic and Katy. He hoped that they had got away alive.

Chapter 19.
The Great Escape

Freezing from the cold, Katy's teeth chattered.

"H-h-how h-has has the water calmed down so quickly?" her voice quivered.

The smaller dolphin swam over to this sad-looking child and very gently explained.

"This once-raging ocean has been transformed into the Sea of Tranquillity, and methinks someone up there is looking after you both."

"I hope it is my Aunt Agatha." Katy cried with pain in her heart at the loving times she had had with her aunt.

The creature had a heavenly face and the water that surrounded him appeared to be like millions of tiny shimmering rays of light, made up of colours that Katy could not ever imagine seeing; it was magical.

"If someone is watching over us, how come they cannot find The Emerald Key for us?" she asked a bemused Dolphin.

"I don't know the answer to that one, my dear, but I am sure everything will turn out right in the end."

"If only Katy was aware of us watching over her and helping her on her treacherous journey."

Agatha looked at Magi for an answer.

"Well, my dear," He coughed as he stroked his long white beard, "your favourite niece would not learn anything if you helped her all the time, now, would she?"

"Yer right, as usual, Magi my old friend, but I cannot stop worrying about her."

"I think we should be worrying more about Art and his newly made friends, as they have a hazardous journey ahead of them."

Magi peered into his trusty oracle and listened carefully as he watched the sad group trapped in the dark waters of Marble Mountain.

Art was still trying to look interested in Ben's story as the young boy proceeded.

"When we souls leave our Earthly body, we go on a journey which will take us to the spirit world which is a planet of beautiful bright light. There are also places called The Halls of Healing where the likes of us broken souls who have suffered pain would normally go to be healed and nursed back to healthy souls, enabling us to enjoy living on the Planet of Light."

Stopping for breath, Ben shuffled on his haunches and continued to tell the story.

"Hang on a minute, I know that," laughed Art. "How do you think I came to be here?"

"Please do not interrupt." Ben was struggling to get his story out.

"I was part of a circus musical act and was on a high wire playing my violin when I slipped off and caused internal injuries to my chest, so I need healing also," Art interrupted again.

"How long have you been here, Art?"

"About three weeks," he replied.

"So, you probably do not know what has happened as we have been trapped down here for nearly two years."

"Go on then, tell me, Ben, I am all ears."

"We have on this planet a wise man called Machu who was the last guardian of the Emerald Key which, by the laws of the planet, should have been delivered by him when he passed over to the spirit world. That should have been his destiny. However, unfortunately, Machu died suddenly in an accident and he was only a young man at the time of his death so he had to make an important decision as to who he gave the precious Key to as it was too soon to be brought to the Planet of Light. There was a lovely lady, Agatha, who nursed him for a long time before he died and he knew that she was a very spiritual being, so Machu the Wiseman chose her to bring the Emerald Key and its magical properties which would bring, amongst other things, everlasting light to the planet.

As this plan went haywire, we now only have an hour of sunshine a day and that will end soon if we do not find the Emerald Key."

Ben stopped for air which was so thin in the cave.

"Hucan, who knew Agatha had died, had been intercepting every soul's journey as he wants the Emerald Key for himself.

We have heard on the grapevine that Agatha was rescued by a good friend who has her tucked away somewhere away from Hucan's reach."

"I will ask you again, why do they want the Emerald Key?" whispered Art impatiently. He had heard some of the story about Machu when he overheard Dominic the Monk explaining to Katy why she was brought to the planet in the first place. Scratching his dirty face, Ben relaxed a bit as he turned to Art to make his words heard.

"To destroy it, as it will restore the light and the Huccanites will not survive as they feed off the dark forces of the moon." Ben shook with fear at the thought of never being able to escape the horrors that would be.

"Flipping 'eck, scary or what? I have only been here a few weeks, so I am glad I wasn't caught."

He laughed.

"What do you mean you have not been caught? You are here with us now, you stupid ninny."

Ben shook his head as he held out his good arm to hug Art.

"Welcome aboard, mate."

Art was embarrassed as the small group stared at him with sympathy in their hopeless-looking eyes.

"So, why are they keeping us here, then? That's what I would like to know." Art was frightened of the reply he might get.

"The Hucan warriors won't last forever, so, we are trapped here in pickled water, so to speak, until we are ready to be trained up as warriors who will reign havoc forevermore if the planet loses its light."

"Well, let me tell you, boy, the Emerald Key is actually here on the Planet of Light but has been stolen."

"What?!" The group screamed. "Has Hucan got it?"

They were petrified and needed to be reassured as they huddled together to comfort one another.

"Now, it is a long story and I think we should be planning our escape first. I will tell you all about it eventually, but first things first."

Boom, boom boom!!!

"What was that? It nearly burst my ruddy eardrums!" yelled Art and he put his hands over his ears to protect them from the noise.

Ben could see how agitated his new friend was.

"Calm down, Art, we are safe while we are under water. It is the warriors who are affected by that sound which is a bell tolling. You must have heard it on the way in here;

anyway, the ringing tone brainwashes anyone who comes into its vicinity. Anyone who escapes has a chance of survival."

Ben gazed into Art's blue eyes and hoped he would be their saviour as he had survived it.

"What effect does it have on the brain, then?"

Art was interested in knowing as Dominic the Monk had guided him and Katy on how to prevent the bell from penetrating their mind.

"It dulls the mind and we become like zombies, unable to think for ourselves, but as I said earlier, we are quite safe under water." "Wow, thank goodness for that." Art was pouring with sweat, relieved at the news.

Splash! Splash! An ugly fish was thrown into the water by one of the Huccanite soldiers. The fish were called Globs. The big-lipped fish was a flesh-eating one and thrashed about in the water violently.

It was overpowered by Art who hung onto it like grim death.

"Hang on, you little squirt, what do you think you are doing?"

The silver and black wriggling fish was taken by surprise and opened its frog-like eyes in panic.

"Hey, I only want a meal. I am starving, and I don't eat much, how about me just having the tip of your little finger? That is not a lot to ask, now, is it? I recognise you, as you are the lunch that I captured earlier."

"Ha, ha!" Art roared with laughter.

"Little flesh-eater, if you play your cards right, we might help you escape with us then you will have all the food you want and you won't have the Soldier Globs ordering you around, making you do what they want you to do. C'mon, how about it, and make it snappy!" Art clicked his fingers waiting for a reply.

"Make it snappy? Huh! I am a fish, not a crocodile and I cannot play cards, only dominoes. Will that make me part of your gang? And by the way, I am Mr Guppy. Pleased to meet you all and watch I don't knock spots of you, ha, ha, excuse the pun."

Art and his friends liked Mr Guppy and decided he could join them in their search for freedom.

Suddenly, Art was conscious of a shadow overlooking them from above the water. It was one of the Glob soldiers who seemed to be listening to their conversation, puzzled by their words.

"Hey, folks up there, can you hear me?" Art was hoping for more support from freedom fighters.

He continued shouting to the shadowy figure.

"I can help us all if you only listen to me."

He wanted to save as many broken souls as possible.

"I am all ears; well, none of us are perfect!" the Glob answered.

The soldier was laughing but inside he was so unhappy, not knowing what Hucan, the leader, had in store for him and the rest of the Huccanite soldiers. Maybe this guy below water had better ideas.

Clambering onto a rock that jutted above the pool, Art lifted his head cautiously above the waterline.

There were a few of the Globs standing there like zombies as that is what they were becoming over time.

He once again took control of the situation and beckoned the Globs closer.

"Gather round and stick together, you lot."

"We are not made of superglue," one strapping individual replied.

The Globs huddled closer to the side of the pool hoping that Hucan and his killer soldiers would not be aware of the plan that was about to unfold.

Art had a crowd around him now and needed to instil in them how important it was for them to work together.

"Teamwork, that's what we want, so if there is anyone out there just thinking about saving their own skin, forget it. It won't work; do you get my drift?"

"We are united," spluttered one of the Globs staring at the rest of his cronies.

"All for one and one for all!" they cried in unison.

"Let us see now." Art scratched his chin as his brain worked overtime on ideas.

"You all know how to meditate, so we will begin."

He was getting excited as he felt a rush of adrenaline.

"Hang on a minute," a voice from the gods responded.

"Mecidate? Mecidate? What the heck is that?" The majority shook their head in ignorance.

Ben was not on his own here as he had no idea whatsoever.

"Meditate, it's called. It is simple really - I will explain as we go along, ok, everyone? Are you all sitting comfortably?" Art felt like a teacher ready to tell a bedtime story.

He studied the crowd of poor souls who were looking to him for guidance and he crossed his fingers for luck.

"Can you rap, and can you sing?" He was in fits of laughter at this stage, tears running down his face, but his friends did not find it funny.

"Of course, we can," Ben answered indignantly, searching through the crowd for support.

"Yes, we can; can you, Mr Guppy?" "Y-yes, I think so." He gulped and whispered, "What about the Globs?"

The Globs were muttering to one another, shaking their heads and looking for reassurance. "We are quick learners so count us in."

"Right, off we go." Art's arms were like the conductor of an Orchestra's baton.

"All together now, sit in the silence and find your inner peace, be at one with yourselves and blot any noise out other than my instructions."

They all sat so serenely, their faces filled with hope and anticipation.

"One, two, three, all together now,
We will meditate,
We will contemplate,
We will lift our minds to a special place.
Rap, rap, rap,
Come on, clap your hands together, friends;
We will get out of this evil den,
Lift our mind and fill it with light,
Cause we will escape from here tonight.

The sad group were clapping and rapping and singing their heads off and eventually, they all felt happier than they had been for a long time.

They had visualised a bright happy place as Art had suggested and it seemed to be working now by lifting up their spirits for a start.

Strangely, the wet and hungry souls, who had all gathered in a circle, began to rise up through the murky sludge and slime.

The Globs were waiting in anticipation as they had also sung and rapped to the beat.

They could not believe it when out of the water rose Art, the lost souls, and Mr Guppy who had a big grin on his face.

They all clung to one another and when they were lifted above the pool, they were all dazzled by the bright light that surrounded them.

"It is working!" screamed Ben, his face lit up like an angel as they approached a plateau of scintillating colours which were now mingled with bright rays of stardust.

It was awesome and they were lost for words for a moment.

"Thank God." They prayed humbly and gave thanks.

"Hip hooray."

They gave Art an encore as they lifted him onto their weary shoulders.

"Well done." They all took turns at slapping him on the back. The Globs were in awe of what had happened and eagerly followed Art and the others.

"Alright, give it a rest; my back is killing me now."

He chuckled as he felt proud of himself.

"Stick with me and I will lead us to the Crystal Caves where I am sure you will meet up with my other friends, hopefully, and pray that all our dreams will be fulfilled."

The now larger group of escaped souls trundled down the sides of the Marble Mountain, their faces shining in the anticipation of all their hopes coming true, as they believed that when they reached the Crystal Cave, miracles would surely happen.

There was a spring in their step; even those who were crippled managed to show how elated they were through cheering all the time.

There was also a flesh-eating fish trailing along at the back of everybody.

"Call me Mr Guppy," he laughed. "I have been converted from a greedy guppy to a goody yuppy guppy and I like it."

Art was deep in thought as he had a lot of responsibility now.

I hope Dominic and Katy have found the Emerald Key to open the Crystal Cave, the souls will have light restored to the planet and to the Halls of Healing making them all whole again. Maybe I am too sure of myself. Art was losing his confidence and sighed as he plodded on regardless.

"Never mind, what will be, will be."

This was more like Art.

Meanwhile, back in Magi the magician's cave, Aunt Agatha was in her usual frenzy of worry.

Chapter 20.
Bristles the Broom

"Wipe the oracle, will you? And be quick."

"Manners, Agatha," Magi reminded bossy boots, who was only like this with him as she was so stressed.

"Sorry, Sir."

The dark orb was, as usual, covered in dust and cobwebs as if it had not been used for a long time.

"Flippin' 'eck, don't you do any dusting around here, Magi?"

Agatha coughed and spluttered as the dust stuck in her throat. She tried to calm herself down, but as usual, her niece was her main topic of worry.

The old magician was just as sick of the dust as his dear friend was and muttered to himself, "*She has been here a year and it has not bothered her until now; women!!*"

Stepping forward and picking up his wand from a dusty shelf, he proceeded to get the cleaners in, so to speak.

"Magic broom, do your stuff, get rid of this blooming dust."

Phsshh wssshhh! The wooden brush came to life after being propped up in the corner for a few hours and he thought he was on holiday. As if!

The broom swept and blew the particles of dust out of the cave entrance, looking for more work to do as Agatha would find more to moan about. The place was immaculate when he finished, just like a new pin. He settled his wooden body back into his corner; he was shattered.

Turning round to Magi, its bushy head full of dust, sweat and tears, Bristles the broom remarked angrily, "Why don't you move, find another dwelling? You know that the dust keeps piling up through the smoke and rubbish from Marble Mountain. Their furnaces never stop. I am flogging a dead horse; every day, all I do is sweep, sweep."
"Instead of sleep, sleep, I suppose," laughed Magi.
"Stop moaning and get on with it.
And where can we move to? Another planet?
Do what you are made for, Bristles."
By this time, Agatha was laughing so hard, tears were running down her face.

Pulling herself together, she immediately checked out the Oracle, which was now like a shining black looking glass, so clean you could see your face in it. Not that Agatha wanted to see her old wrinkly face in it. She sniggered at the thought.

"Is that better?" Magi smiled and waited for a reaction from his good friend.

"Good job, well done! So, now I can still watch from a distance making sure that my beloved Katy is safe from harm. Anyway, Magi, put the kettle on and please make some blueberry tea and space cakes smothered in strawberry jam, yum."

She licked her lips in anticipation, so pleased that Magi had the sense to pick fruits months ago and store them before the light began to fade from the planet.

"Good thinking, Batman." Agatha rubbed her fat tummy and sat back waiting for her lunch while watching what Katy was up to.

Bristles sulked in the corner. He never got any treats and the only friend he had was a dustpan. *Oh well, I think I will brush up on my chatting up instead of sweeping up*, he chuckled.

Peering into the oracle, Agatha was ready for her rescue work if it was needed.

She was ever so grateful to her once email friend, now good friend, Magi, for stepping in to help her when she was on her journey as the Hucan would have stepped in and she would have been no more.

He had protected her as she would also do for Katy.

The elderly lady was safe here until it was time to leave for the Halls of Healing.

"Now, where are you, Katy? When did we see you last?"

"From sharks to dolphins, I believe. My spell worked a treat."

Magi puffed his chest out proudly.

"Oh yes, it will be sink or swim for Dominic and Katy."

Aunt Agatha hoped that the spell cast was successful in saving these two lovely people.

Chapter 21.
Dolphins and Rainbow Fairy

As the blue dolphins swam through the water gracefully, they sang to each other in a high-pitched tone, and it was absolutely magical, thought Katy, like tiny bells tinkling on a light breeze.

She felt safe with them and as she peered back, she could see the look of peace on Dominic's face.

"Now I know why it's called the Sea of Tranquillity."

As she leaned over sideways, the waves gently splashed her dirty face, washing away the muck and dust that had accumulated over the last few weeks.

The last time she had felt this secure was when she was in Aunt Agatha's arms.

The poor bedraggled figure broke down and cried as she sent out lots of love and light for her aunt, her family and all the broken souls on this dying planet.

"God, I was a right little devil to everyone, especially my brother and sister.

Please forgive me," she prayed, hoping someone would hear her.

Deep down, Katy was beginning to understand all the mumbo jumbo about souls living on another planet and hoped that she could make their dreams come true by helping all she could.

Maybe it will make up for the grief I caused on Mother Earth, she thought.

The dolphins were in their element as they glided through the sea, glad that they were able to help these lovely people to escape to a better place.

One of the beautiful creatures knew that there was a small island not too far away where they would take Dominic and Katy as it would be a sanctuary for them.

After a long time on this wondrous journey, the larger dolphin smiled and announced, "We are here now, folks. We will slow down, and you can both swim to land as the water is too shallow for us to continue; we would be stranded."

"We understand and will be in your debt for ever."

Dominic patted their heads. "Thank you from the bottom of our hearts. Go on, Katy, show your appreciation."

The tired monk tried to encourage the nine-year-old but she was very hesitant and did not want anyone to know just how caring she was.

"Bye!" She waved and swam away from the dolphins with Dominic in tow as he was not a great swimmer.

As Katy turned back to the dolphins, the sea washed away her tears, tears of sorrow.

She wanted to show she cared but her heart still felt cold like a block of ice since her loving aunt had left her.

What would it take for her to feel love again, she wondered sadly?

"Thank you." Her voice was carried on the wind to the happy dolphins who winked at one another as they knew that the young girl's block of ice was slowly beginning to melt.

She was unaware of it.

Shaking the cold seawater from her wet clothes, Katy stood in amazement at her surroundings.

"I don't believe it; what a beautiful place! So peaceful and so spiritual." She was mesmerised by the scene.

The grass was so green and soft underfoot and there were flowers of all colours and a ginormous old, gnarled fruit tree swaying and rustling in the warm breeze.

"Dominic, have you ever seen trees as big as these?"

"Sorry." Of course, he was blind.

The branches tinkled in the wind as they walked past it, so Dominic stretched out his hand to feel the texture of the leaves and breathed in the wonderful perfume emanating from it.

Katy was in awe of the sight and described it in detail to this lovely man.

They soon came across a clearing in the woods where there were some rocks sticking out of the mossy ground; they looked like stools carved out of the wonderful rock.

"Let's sit down for a while and get our breath back. Pick a seat, Dom."

The weary couple found a comfy round-shaped rock and sat down carefully.

"Ahhh, a rest at last." Katy looked at Dominic's kind face knowing he was a special person. However, she never, ever mentioned it. That was Katy.

"I think it is time for something to eat, what do you say, my girl?"

Katy did not have time to reply as she heard a rustling in the nearby bushes.

"Boo, hoo, what can we do?"

A cry came from the undergrowth of plants and bracken.

As Katy moved the leaves, there on a toadstool sat a tiny delicate fairy with wings that shimmered in the rays of the sun.

"Your wings," Katy said in amazement, "are like the colours of the rainbow; they are magnificent."

"Waahhh! Waah!" The little creature was distressed even more.

"Don't mention rainbow to me or my other mates," she sobbed uncontrollably, her tears soaking into her gossamer gown.

"Why, whatever is the matter?" Katy asked earnestly, not wanting to cause any more harm to this little being.

"My friends and I have forgotten the colours of the rainbow, and Rainbow Warrior will go ballistic when he finds out. Oh, help us, somebody, anybody." She sounded desperate.

Flit the fairy was so distressed that she had created a puddle of tears around her.

Suddenly, about twenty other tiny creatures emerged from the undergrowth, elves, pixies, goblins, butterflies and small insects, all ready to help in any way they could.

"None of us have the answer, Flit. We have been racking our brains for days now and cannot get it right, and we are running out of time as the sun only comes out for an hour a day."

The sun had only just come out in the last half hour and Katy realised that, without it, this gathering of miniature beings would not be as colourful.

"Richard of York gave battle in vain," whispered Katy.

"What are you going on about, dude? DOH!" A goblin was annoyed now.

A pixie stared at the outburst of this young girl.

"Are you right in the head or what?"

They all started to roll around laughing at red-faced Katy.

"Don't be embarrassed, my dear."

Dominic placed his hand on the blushing nine-year-old's shoulders to comfort her.

"Ger off, ya muppet. I am not embarrassed, I am flippin' red with anger," growled Katy.

"Listen to me, ya bunch of idiots." She stuck her chest out like a peacock and appeared to be pleased with herself.

"I have just given you the colours of the rainbow; what more do you want, jam on it?"

"No, I don't like jam; the colours will do." The butterfly swooped up and down excitedly.

"I-I don't like jam either," whispered a shy little dragonfly hovering slowly behind a pixie.

They all roared with laughter as the insect went scarlet.

"Shame you were not a red admiral butterfly." They laughed even more at Katy's sarcastic comment.

"Attention, everyone," Katy shouted to make sure her audience heard her every word.

You could hear a pin drop it was so quiet. She began her so-called recipe.

Richard	Red
Of	Orange
York	Yellow
Gave	Green

Battle	Blue
In	Indigo
Vain	Violet

"Do you understand, you dimwits?"

They gazed at her cocky face and appeared to be puzzled.

It suddenly dawned on them. "Richard of York gave battle in vain. Yes, what a lovely way to remember the colours," giggled Flit the fairy.

"Glad the penny has dropped," Katy joked.

"What penny?" a voice from the gods shouted.

"Never mind; it will take too long to explain and the sun will have dimmed by then, a bit like you lot." She could not resist. That was Katy for you.

"Hurrah! Pleased to meet you, lady. You are our friend for life."

"Quickly, we have less than half an hour till the sun stops shining…"

Gonzo the goblin hurried them along and the tiny area of plant life became a busy beehive.

They were racing against time now as the light of the sun became fainter.

The fairies flitted from one flower to another, squeezing the colours out of the petals while the butterflies mixed it with nectar.

The goblins placed each individual colour into the shells of horse chestnuts and carefully laid them side by side.

"What is all the panic about?"

Dominic was concerned at the urgency of it all.

"We have heard a whisper on the grapevine that the sun is actually going to die forever, and this planet will be destroyed, unless, of course, there is a miracle."

Goblin wiped a tear from his cheek and stifled his sobs.

"And Rainbow Warrior, who is our boss man, is coming to visit us later today and he would go crackers if he knew that we had lost the formula for the rainbow as we need all the help we can get in saving this planet, so thank you from the bottom of our hearts."

Gonzo blushed as he had never made a long speech before.

"We are not aware of your leader, Rainbow Warrior, but we will do all we can to contribute as Katy, who is an Earthling, was sent here on a great mission, believe me. I am a blind soul with other issues that require healing also.

Anyway, our main priority is to bring the light back to this beautiful planet of yours."

The tired monk winked as Katy crossed her fingers for luck.

Katy smiled! Katy smiled! That was a big improvement.

"Now, which way to the Crystal Cave? Let me remember." Dominic racked his brain while scratching his head.

Katy glared at him. "But you don't have the Emerald Key yet, you idiot. I am sorry, Dom; me and my big mouth. I forget that you are an old man." She was ashamed. That's an improvement.

Old, old Dominic laughed to himself. "I am only forty-eight, but that probably seems like a lifetime to a nine-year-old.

He accepted her apology as he sat down on a large toadstool.

"I will have to sit in the silence to see if I can get some direction."

He made himself comfortable as he drank his lunar shake, which Flit the fairy had made for him with moon mallow plant and juniper juice poured into the petals of harebells that were shaped like cups.

"Delicious."

He wiped his lips with his catkin napkin.

Katy sat in the silence too, thinking of her family and how much she missed them, wishing she had treated them better, and hoping they were all ok.

She blinked her eyes nervously and her mind reflected on happier times, and then Art popped into her thoughts. Where was he with his silly sense of humour? She could not believe that she missed him too.

I hope he is safe, bless him.

Her heart was very slowly opening to caring about others and the block of ice was slowly melting a drip at a time. "Where are you, Art?" She sat and prayed silently.

Katy realised that people were especially important to her. She was annoyed at letting her feelings get in the way.

"C'mon, stupid, pull yourself together," she whispered.

Chapter 22.
Long Trek

"Have we got far to go now? I am really tired and fed up."

Mr Guppy dragged his tail along the grassy bank of a river which they had come to and he plopped down to take a dip and a sip in the cool water which helped recharge them all.

"When the rainbow appears in the sky, that will be the end of our journey," mumbled Ben, not really believing that they would ever see their dreams come true.

"Rainbow, rainbow, we don't have enough sunshine or rain to make a blinking rainbow; what a load of codswallop," one of the Globs exclaimed as he was at the end of his tether and running out of patience.

"Codswallop? What is that when it's at sea?" piped up Mr Guppy inquisitively.

"Have you no brains, Guppy? It means rubbish; have you got that?"

"I am not a dustbin man and yes, I get it, Gobby Globby."

The onlookers howled with hysterical laughter. The journey was worth it just for all the fun they were having along the way and it lifted their dying spirits.

Art repeated Ben's story of Aunt Agatha being chosen to bring the Emerald Key.

"This plan went haywire, but to answer your question of the rainbow, the sun creates humidity as it soaks up the rain which has fallen and then shines its light onto the droplets of rain creating the rainbow, however, with only short bursts of sunshine, you have no rainbow."

"Hopefully, when my friends Katy and Dominic find the ancient Key and can do what they have to do at the Crystal Caves, then the rainbow will appear in the sky, enabling us to use it as a bridge to the Halls of Healing, where we will all be made whole again in mind, body and spirit."

Art prayed inwardly that it would all work out to plan or they would all be doomed.

"What do we do once we are better, then? Cause I get fed up if I am hanging around with nothing to do."

Mr Guppy waited for an answer.

"You will not have time to be bored," Ben replied as he rubbed one of his heels which had blistered during the long trek.

"We will all live in peace, harmony, love and joy here on the Planet of Light, helping others to enjoy our beautiful resting place where we will want for nothing.

There will be lots of colours, flowers, precious stones, music, dance, art and plenty of creative pursuits, if you want to pursue them, of course, and food will be plentiful once the light is restored."

"Thanks for that." Mr Guppy smiled sheepishly. Funny that, considering he was a fish!

Onward they trekked, and even though they knew that the Crystal Cave was still a great distance away, they wearily carried on, knowing it would all be worth the effort in the end.

The weary group was absolutely shattered as they had been travelling a long time on foot and had little strength left.

They had all become subdued, and some appeared to be worried.

What if there is no light? What if there is no rainbow?

"God, help us." Art put his hands together and prayed, his friends following suit.

As he was praying, he thought he heard a voice that seemed to be far away, so he held up his hand to halt the group.

"Where is my darling Katy? Please, if anyone can hear us, our life is in a terrible mess. Please help us."

The voice faded away, sobbing, as it became fainter and fainter.

Art's sensitivity told him the message was from Mother Earth.

"Yes, indeed. Where is Katy?" he reflected sadly, eager to find her safe along with Dominic the Monk.

Chapter 23.
Court Hearing

Katy's mum, Natalie, had been to a counsellor for stress therapy, hoping it would help her; she did not want to take medication as it could be addictive.

She had a busy day ahead of her as they were due in court later and knew that David and herself had a tough fight on their hands against Richard Bex.

"Wish you were here, Aunt Agatha; we miss you so much and we know you would have supported us through this." David squeezed her hand to reassure her.

Her eyes were red raw through crying and she had not slept since Katy had gone missing.

"The great creator is teaching us a lesson, David; we should have given Katy more love and attention." Nat wept.

"But Nat, we do love her, it's just that we had a lot to cope with since Aunt Agatha died, and we never seemed to find the time. I hope we are fortunate enough to be given a second chance to make it up to her," sighed David.

"Please forgive us and keep her safe, and hopefully we will still have a home for her with love in our hearts - lots of it."

They made their way to court with a dark cloud hanging over them as they were so negative of the outcome.

The judge appeared to be very sombre as he read the paperwork in front of him, and as he scrutinized Aunt Agatha's Will, he rubbed his chin while gazing towards the loving couple in front of him.

They were holding onto each other for support, both shaking like jelly on a plate.

"Hmm, I am afraid, Mr and Mrs Bex, that this young man has the legal rights to your aunt's estate, and unfortunately, you will have to move out of the property and find alternative accommodation, unless you can find another Will that was made after this one leaving it all to yourselves."

The now deathly pale couple knew there was no other Will as they had turned Maple Manor upside down searching through Aunt Agatha's personal belongings.

They had to accept the Judge's decision.

"When do we have to leave our home, well, the Manor House?" David trembled as he felt their foundations being ripped from under them.

"The sooner the better!" screeched Cocky Richard Bex across the courtroom, his face twisted in anger.

"Tomorrow won't come soon enough for me," he squealed.

"Ahem!" the judge coughed. "Silence in court.

I know you want this sorted out immediately, Mr Bex, and I would normally agree, however, I have to allow this couple and their children a month to move out of your property as we do not want them to be homeless, now do we?"

The judge's sweet smile annoyed Richard Bex.

Shaking his fist, he jumped up in anger.

"What about the monies in the bank? That is mine as well! I want it sorted now, judge man."

"No, calm down, Mr Bex. The monies owed to you will be kept in a private account until this case is completed, which will be in a month's time."

"I am not happy about this as I want to…"

Richard got no further as the judge dismissed the case until further notice.

"Four weeks from today then, thank you."

The judge tidied the papers on his desk, then slowly rose from his chair. "Good day."

Everyone filed out of court, the nosey ones watching the young emotional couple trying to hold back the tears.

"Get us away from here, David, before I crack up."

Nat found it hard to compose herself as the tears flowed.

No house and no money; but that was the least of their problems, even though it was a big one.

Reaching out to her husband, Nat cried, "Where are you, my darling Katy? I don't care about material things, David, I just want our daughter back."

They both wept.

The courtroom had been packed with nearly everyone from the village and they were overly concerned and hoped the judge would be on this lovely family's side, but that was not to be and they would be out on the streets as Richard Bex had the Will to prove it and had won the case.

As if they didn't have enough to worry about! Katy was now classed as a missing person and the police expected to find the body of this young girl as they had searched the homes and the surrounding areas of the village and had interviewed a lot of people.

Sadie Frost had been under suspicion at first, but the police realized that Sadie was not a killer, just a bully, which was bad enough.

The police did not know that all the interviews with Sadie had given her the biggest fright of her life, and she made a promise never to bully anyone again.

"I hope you are safe, Katy Bex."

Sadie had been sending out prayers every night.

"I must give that stupid pink bag back to the Bex family, as it may be all they have left of Katy. Oh God, forgive me." Sadie dragged the bag out from under the floorboards and set off to Maple Manor hoping that the Bex's were back from court.

She was tapping into her guilt and that was making her a nicer person bringing out the best in herself at last.

"C'mon, sweetheart, let's get you home."

David helped his distraught wife into their large saloon car and sped off, away from the courts and the crowds, wondering if the police had any news on Katy.

Inspector Leyland was treating this case as serious as Katy had been missing for well over a week and there was no information on her whereabouts.

"It does not look good, Sergeant Myers. Hope nothing bad has happened to the wee girl."

"Now, Inspector, that's not like you. We must remain positive and keep an open mind."

"Suppose so," he replied as he filled more report forms out for the unsolved case.

He rubbed the stubble on his chin. "Mmm, could do with a shave. Now, where do we go from here?" He shuffled through Katy's case papers, deep in thought.

"She couldn't vanish off the face of the Earth, could she?"

Sergeant Myers shrugged his shoulders.

If only they knew how close it was to the truth.

Chapter 24.
Emerald Key

"Rainbow of colours orange to blue, we can make it all thanks to you.

We take the petals, with nectar we blend.

We love you forever; we thank you our friend.

The little forest creatures sang happily as they had recovered their lost ingredients for their special recipe.

"Bye, Katy; nice to have met you."

"Bye." The young girl lingered as she felt sad. Would she see them again?

Katy was jolted back into reality due to a sound from not far away.

"Shush! What is that? Is it hundreds of birds flying this way?"

She looked at Dominic for guidance, but he was not sure as they both turned their heads to the skies and were pleasantly confronted with the magnificent sight of a white unicorn with beautiful silver wings shimmering in what remained of the dimming sunlight.

As Katy explained the vision to Dominic in detail, the wonderful creature glided towards them slowly, preparing to land.

As Katy had described it all so well, it dawned on Dominic who it was.

"Purity, my friend! I have not seen you in years."

He was overcome with emotion as he ran towards the unicorn who was out of breath after her long flight.

"You're blind, you stupid muppet, so how would you have ever seen him to know who it was?"

Katy was taking the mickey out of the jubilant monk, but first, he must make things clear to cheeky lovable Katy.

"Purity is not a he, but a female and I have not always been blind. It only happened when our planet lost most of its light as I have ultra-sensitive eyes."

"So, if we find the Emerald Key, will you get your sight back and will they mend your spine? I noticed that it is curved as you stumble sometimes; sorry, Dom."

She felt guilty now and her face reddened.

"Not *if* we find it, but *when* we find it, because we will."

The tired monk did not realise how near they were to obtaining the Emerald Key but had remained positive throughout the journey they had both made.

"And yes, I hope to be able to see again," he whispered.

In all the fuss, they had not been introduced to Minkey and the monkey did not like to be left out. The brown woolly ball of fuzz unfolded and stretched his long arms out as he yawned.

"Hi, my name is Minkey, and you will be ever so pleased that I am here."

He had a twinkle in his eye and patted the parcel of leaves that was still tied to his leg.

Bemused by the monkey, Katy peered closer to his leg to examine it and mockingly said "Why, have you hurt yourself?"

"No, I wrap leaves around my leg for the fun of it, you stupid persona."

Katy's face went purple with temper and she made a lunge for Minkey.

Dominic quickly grabbed Katy to calm her down.

"Now, Minkey," said Purity, licking the monkey's head.

"Do not keep these two lovely people in suspense any longer - tell them the good news, there's a good boy."

"Why should I and what's in it for me?" he yelled.

"Take notice, Minkey," said Purity as she pointed towards Dominic.

"This gentleman is The Keeper of Dreams, guardian of the Crystal Caves. Dominic is also a dear old friend of mine."

"Guardian of the Crystal Caves? Crikey!" Minkey was ecstatic.

Jumping up and down, he eventually unwrapped the package carefully, savouring every minute of Katy's puzzled look, as she stared on in wonder.

There it was in all its glory. The necklace glittered in the fading sunlight as Minkey passed it hesitantly to Dominic.

Purity reassured him that it was in safe hands.

"The Emerald Key! Aunt Agatha's precious necklace!"

Katy had suddenly come to life, her cheeks flooded with colour and her blue eyes sparkling like diamonds.

"Dominic, you know what this means?"

She grabbed hold of the monk and hugged him till it hurt.

"Yes, my dearest girl. I am so delighted knowing that all the ailing souls, including myself, will be healed and made whole again. The planet will be restored with light and will survive, and I will be able to see all the wonderful flowers, birds, animals, skies and, last but not least, your lovely little face, my friend Katy. Oh, I am so grateful to Minkey." Dominic was overcome with emotion.

"Grateful, you say? Wait till you see your friend's face; she reminds me of an old hag." Minkey rolled about in hysterics but was overjoyed knowing that he would have contributed towards helping hundreds of sick souls and their planet. Minkey passed the key to the smiling monk, who placed it gently into the folds of his dirty brown robes, eager to make the journey to the Crystal Caves.

While all this was going on, Flit the fairy and her friends had been watching and listening to all.

"Can we come with you, up Glass Mountain to the Crystal Caves? Please, Mr Dominic?" Their faces were ecstatic with happiness.

Before Dominic had time to answer, a tall shadow fell across them and they lifted their eyes upwards.

There, in all his splendour, stood a magnificent giant of a Red Indian with a full headdress of black and white feathers and a soft buckskin tunic with shell, beads, bones and feathers attached to it. He had his bow and arrow slung over his back, and a tomahawk was tucked into his broad leather belt.

"Where do you think you are going without my permission, my little ones?"

His voice boomed through the trees and Katy was sure she felt the ground vibrate.

The monk stepped forward. "I am Dominic. Pleased to meet you, sir, and your name is?"

The Red Indian, who stood about seven feet tall, crossed his muscular arms in front of him and replied.

"I am Rainbow Warrior, and these are my lovely little soul family. I am happy to know you, my friend."

As Rainbow Warrior towered over these strangers, he was puzzled as to why they were here, in his part of the woods, with his people.

"If you have the time to tell me, Father Dominic?" The Red Indian was interested.

When Dominic's story was over, Rainbow Warrior admired them for their strength of character and perseverance in searching for the Emerald Key.

Flit the fairy felt that Rainbow Warrior needed to be told the truth about them losing the rainbow colour recipe and proceeded to explain the help that Katy had given them in finding it again.

He was so impressed. "I thank you both, and remember, I owe you one." He stood back proudly as he announced;

"We will all go up the Glass Mountain to Crystal Caves and give our support to these two wonderful people, not forgetting Purity and Minkey, as, without them, we would not have the Emerald Key." Minkey felt important for the first time ever. Bless him.

A loud cheer rang through the forest. "Hip, hip, hooray!"

Talking of hips, the sooner mine are mended the better, Rainbow Warrior thought as they were so painful when he walked, but he pretended that everything was ok.

They did not have that far to walk; just as well as they were all tired and the sun had gone down fast, being replaced suddenly with the silver moon which was a full moon and helped them to see their way ahead.

"Wow, no wonder it is called Glass Mountain!" exclaimed the shattered nine-year-old as she rubbed the dust from her eyes.

The mountain was so slippery that it seemed to take forever to reach the top. However, the long trail of souls, elementals, birds with broken wings and tiny creatures emerged at the top feeling battered and bruised after the many tumbles they had encountered, but elation soon replaced their pains, for on the pinnacle of the mountain sat a triangular structure.

The Crystal Cave was a sight to behold. It shimmered in the light of the moon. The many hues and shades of colour radiating from it were iridescent.

It resembled a pyramid-shaped diamond crystal sparkling in all its glory.

"Woo, aahh, ohhh," they whispered, as they were astonished by the brilliant scintillating jewelled temple and approached it humbly.

There in the centre, at the front of the Crystal Cave, was a golden gate embellished with precious crystals which tinkled in the soft breeze.

Dominic fell to his knees in prayer and thanked the angels, one of course being Aunt Agatha. "Don't forget Magi."

They looked around for the invisible voice and gave thanks.

As Dominic, the Keeper of Dreams, fumbled to place the Emerald Key into the ornate lock, he realized that it would not go in without a struggle.

"If at first you don't succeed, try, try, and try again," the crowd chanted, egging him on with their excitement. The

Key refused to go in, and Dominic struggled and dropped it and it fell heavily onto rugged rocks.

"Sorry," he said as if the Key had feelings.

A rolled-up piece of parchment suddenly shot out of the barrel of the Emerald Key and Katy bent forward to pick it up. Her eyes widened with wonder at what it could be, not knowing of the turn of events it would bring.

She suddenly saw a vision of Sadie Frost in her mind - strange, as she had never given Sadie a second thought all the time she was on the Planet of Light.

"It is Aunt Agatha or Mum that I think about constantly." Katy was overcome with sadness.

Chapter 25.
Katy's Book and the Inspector

"I pinched her silly pink bag because it was the one her aunt gave to her, not because I really wanted it. Anyway, here; you can have it.

The only thing in it is some crappy book that belonged to her precious Aunt Agatha; seems like a load of hocus pocus to me."

Throwing the bag to Nat, Sadie Frost quickly walked away without looking back as she still felt guilty at the way she treated people. "Will I ever change?" she sighed.

Katy's mum, Nat, went straight back into the house and phoned the police station.

"I will come straight away, sir."

Ten minutes later, she appeared at the station, the book clutched tightly in her hand.

"Thanks for bringing this in, Mrs Bex, as every little bit of information can help."

Inspector Leyland flicked through the old brown leather-bound book, which was about six inches by four inches big, and seemed to have lots of healing remedies written down by Agatha, Nat assumed.

However, the Inspector knew this book was ancient as so many of the wise healers had written their remedies in it.

At the back, there were lots of email addresses, some sounding out of this world. The Inspector chuckled to himself.

"Listen to this, Sarge.

"Crystal Clear, Harmony Healing, Magi Keeper of Dreams @ oracle.cloud.air.

What is that all about? Mmm, must follow this up. It might give us some clues; besides, there were many other emails too.

Sergeant Myers, I have a job for you up at Maple Manor.

Pronto."

"Ok, boss." The sergeant had his jacket on in seconds, ready to go.

James led the young policeman upstairs. "Yes, Sir. Aunt Agatha's computer is still where she left it, in her study, Angel's Den. I will show you."

James was eager to help as he really missed his younger sister and wanted to be of assistance.

He offered to show the sergeant the ins and outs of the computer.

Numerous cups of coffee and sandwiches and four hours later, they decided to call it a day, when, out of the blue, something appeared on the screen without being prompted.

Activate crystal ball to save the Planet of Light.

The words flashed several times, and the sergeant could not understand it at all.

"Turn it off, son; what a load of rubbish."

Turning the computer off, they left the study, closing the door gently behind them.

The crystal ball which was on the desk pulsated with a luminous green light and there, once again, a message appeared on the computer screen.

"TO CRYSTAL CLEAR.............. MISSION ACCOMPLISHED.

PLANET OF LIGHT FOREVER IN YOUR DEBT.

AGATHA AND MAGI, KEEPER OF DREAMS

@ORACLE.CLOUD.AIR.

The computer logged off automatically.

Meanwhile, on the Planet of Light, the Oracle cave was awake.

"Now, Magi, how is Katy coping? Has she made the wonderful discovery yet?" Agatha prayed.

Chapter 26.
Rainbow Bridge

"What's this?" Katy picked up the roll of yellow parchment and unfurled it. Reading it slowly, Katy's face went white at the words written on the parchment. She could not understand this and rolled it back up as she looked at the crowd around her, watching her every move.

She placed it in her pyjama pocket saying nothing to her friends, who were staring at her, wondering why she had gone pale and silent. Katy did not know that some of her special friends were psychic.

Her silence was caused by shock.

"Where there's a Will, there's a way." Flit the fairy giggled.

"And where there's a Will, there's a relative." Rainbow Warrior winked.

Katy remained quiet.

The crowd fell about laughing.

"Now for the most important part; let us try again to open the gate."

Dominic's hand shook.

As if by magic, the golden gate opened, unlocking dreams and wishes made by all.

Everyone was overcome with emotion and were hugging each other with love and happiness. They were so glad to be free; free from the darkness that had enveloped the planet and free of their illnesses as the Halls of Healing would be able to use the sun's rays to make them well again.

As the sun lit up the skies, all the colours of the flowers and plants came to life. They were radiant as they opened to the warmth of the sun's rays. You could hear trees creaking as they unfurled their branches and opened their leaves, embracing the wonderful sunshine.

Rainbow Warrior did a rain dance and soon, tiny pear-shaped droplets of rain cascaded down on the dry soil bringing the parched plants to life.

You could feel the vibration of the plants absorbing the much-needed energy of the life-giving rainwater.

"Three cheers for the Keeper of Dreams - Hip, hip, hooray!"

"Now, I did not do it on my own." The old monk was embarrassed.

"We have Katy to thank as she was the one who brought the Emerald Key to the Planet of Light."

The crowd were euphoric as they agreed.

"Well done, Katy! For she's a jolly good fellow," they chanted till they were hoarse.

Katy blushed and asked, "Why are there two rainbows in the sky?"

She was mesmerised as she turned to her friend, the Red Indian, waiting for a reply.

He placed his hand fondly on Katy's shoulder.

"Earthlings usually come here to the Planet of Light just once, but you have to return as your life on Earth is not over yet. Both rainbows are like escalators; we have one coming up, and just for you, we have one going back down. You are incredibly special, Katy Bex, and don't ever forget it. You healed the planet for millions of souls, and we will be forever grateful, dear child."

She did not reply as she was choked up with feelings that she had not felt for a long time.

As she turned away from Rainbow Warrior, Katy saw a throng of souls not too far away but didn't give it a second thought, not realising it was Art and his many friends.

"Hey guys, what did I tell you? There's the rainbow; in fact, there is another one too. Unusual, though." Ben was breaking into a run now and the group followed in anticipation.

Those that could run were running, screaming, laughing, shouting and crying as every emotion came out as they sped towards the rainbows and the queues of souls waited at the beginning of the beautifully coloured arch of many colours.

Art spotted Dominic and sprinted towards him and Katy, who had seen him.

There were hugs of joy and tears as Art and Katy clung to each other and the monk knew that Art would remain a friend for eternity.

"C'mon, Katy, no more tears. You have a journey to make back to Earth - just think of the brilliant welcome you will get as you will have been missed so much, I am sure,"

Dominic reassured the tearful young girl, who was crying for her family, and for the wonderful souls she had met and felt love for.

The three friends walked over to the second rainbow, the one descending to Earth like a bridge, and once again, they hugged Katy.

"It is not as if we will not see one another again, is it?" shrieked Art.

"Talking about seeing each other, you are beautiful, my girl, just as I imagined."

Dominic's warm brown eyes were brimming over.

"Dom, you are not blind anymore! I am so pleased for you."

The nine-year-old Katy gently squeezed the monk's hand and felt so sad at leaving these good friends.

"You are right, Art. Of course, we will see each other one day, so, in the meantime, when I go back home, I will do my best at school and will help other people the best way I can. After all, we are all the same, no matter what creed, colour or disability."

"Yes, my child, we all come from the same source and we all return to that source, which is pure love; always remember that."

Dominic kissed Katy's cheeks which were wet with tears.

Rainbow Warrior looked on with a big grin on his face.

"Don't know why I did a rain dance when you guys have got bucketsful of water here." They all chuckled together.

"Goodbye and God bless, young lady."

Art and Dominic held back their emotions now as this young girl had certainly changed for the better.

As Katy stepped onto the rainbow, she saw something leggy clambering up the other rainbow which was ascending.

She could not believe it; Silky the spider was whole again as he waved to her and blew a kiss, his long eyelashes fluttering under the lovely sunshine. Katy was overjoyed.

There was also a lone figure, as large as life, an African gentleman.

"Thank you from the bottom of my heart," he shouted to Katy.

"It is I, Machu, the wise man. God bless you as I have been waiting to heal these poor souls for nearly a year now and you made it possible."

"My pleasure, Machu, and I am sure Aunt Agatha had a lot to do with it," she replied.

Out of the mist behind Machu stepped her beloved Aunt Agatha, who was now a picture of health.

"Love you to the moon and back, Katy; never forget it."

Katy could feel her aunt's arms enfolding her from a distance and suddenly she sensed the overwhelming warmth in her heart. The block of ice around her heart had melted. She could experience love again and was elated at having contact with her loving aunt.

"By the way, Katy, this is Magi. He helped you and me along the way." Magi waved to Katy while stroking his beard as usual.

Waving goodbye once again, Katy's attention was brought back by a massive explosion in the distance.

"Marble Mountain and the Hucan are no more. The curse has been lifted from our planet," Machu shouted for all to hear. "And we will keep the Emerald Key here in its rightful place for us to treasure. "Goodbye, my dear." He waved and blew a kiss which was in the form of a long ray of dancing stardust.

"Goodbye!" Katy would miss them all.

There were hundreds of happy souls ascending towards the Halls of Healing; some had already been healed with the strong sunlight.

Chapter 27.
Home Sweet Home

Katy woke up feeling ever so refreshed. Throwing off the fluffy pink duvet, she jumped out of her comfortable warm bed and slipped her feet into her pink slippers.

She rubbed the sleep out of her eyes as she frowned and gazed around her bedroom, feeling like a stranger.

"Flippin' 'eck! That was some dream I had - or was it a nightmare?"

The youngster looked bewildered as she walked downstairs with a puzzled look on her face and yelled, "Mum, Dad, are you up yet? What the heck is this up my sleeve?" she muttered, withdrawing the yellow parchment, but too hungry to read it as she went towards the kitchen.

"Did you hear Katy's voice or am I losing the plot?"

Nat stared into David's blue eyes with hope, praying for a miracle.

David could not answer his shocked wife as he thought he was also hearing things.

The door of the kitchen opened, and Katy stood there with an angelic smile that would melt the hardest heart.

"Good morning! What a dream I have just had. I cannot understand it, and what is this rolled-up piece of paper doing up the sleeve of my pyjama top? Filthy scary or what?"

She handed it to David." Throw it in the bin, Dad. It looks like rubbish."

As he unfurled the scroll of paper and scrutinised every word, he passed it to Nat and sat back watching her expression change from bewilderment to joy.

Agatha and Magi watched excitedly from afar as the Bex's hugged their daughter so much that Katy thought that they had both had a brainstorm, as she was not used to the fuss.

After her parents got over their shock, they sat down and relayed everything that had happened that was threatening their whole way of life. Their daughter was a God-sent miracle! David eventually read the Will out to his family.

I, AGATHA BEX, BEQUEATH ALL MY MONIES AND PROPERTIES TO MY NEPHEW, DAVID BEX, AND HIS FAMILY.

THIS MAKES ANY OTHER WILL NULL AND VOID.

It had been signed by Aunt Agatha and a nurse at the hospital where she had passed away.

They could not believe their good fortune.

"We not only got our beautiful daughter back, Nat, but our lovely home, Maple Manor, which is filled with our wonderful memories of Aunt Agatha, bless her.

Now we can get on with our lives."

Katy was so mixed up and looked back on her past, thinking:

Is that what Aunt Agatha was trying to tell me, her Will was in The Emerald Key?

What has happened why am I so confused? Oh, never mind, I have had a great sleep; now for breakfast.

There were celebrations in the household and the village lasting for over a week.

"Top grades for the most outstanding pupil in the school go to Katy Bex!"

Nat and David beamed with pride for their eleven-year-old daughter, who was delighted as the teacher presented merit after merit with distinction to her and also praising her with these words:

"My, my, Katy, do you realise that you can do anything you want in any career of your choice, from a lawyer to a banker? You deserve it as you have performed excellent work. Well done."

Miss waited for Katy's response as the beautiful young girl gazed upwards to the ceiling.

Suddenly, there appeared a white mist and her Aunt Agatha's face was surrounded by it.

She was shaking her head from side to side.

Her aunt smiled and said, "How boring! Sorry, Katy, but we have other plans for you, my pet."

As Aunt Agatha's face faded away, the child grinned and vaguely remembered a monk and someone in a colourful cloak. Deep in thought, she murmured, "I will be ready."

She was raring to go on another adventure.

The End

Printed in Great Britain
by Amazon